Egyptian Shifters

MARISA CHENERY

CONTENTS

TURQUOISE EYE OF HORUS

Codie had her trip to Egypt all planned out, but her plans soon fall apart when she gets lost in the Eastern Desert during a sand storm. All alone, she unintentionally calls out to the Egyptian god Horus, whose eye she wears around her neck as a pendant.

Horus comes to Codie in her dreams. The only place he can come to her as a man without drawing his uncle's spiteful attention. Unable to watch Codie suffer during her waking hours, Horus takes his falcon form and goes to her in the mortal realm to watch over her until a rescue party comes.

As Codie's plight worsens, Horus confronts Seth, who has trapped her in the desert to draw Horus out. With their feud as old as time, Horus must defeat Seth if he is to save the mortal woman he wants as his mate.

1

CHAPTER ONE

Codie Marks was hopelessly lost. Just thinking about it sent a shiver of unease running down her spine. Being lost in Egypt's Wadi el Gemal National Park, in the Eastern Desert, could not in any way be considered an ideal situation for a lone Canadian woman to be in.

She had planned this trip for months. She had scrimped and saved every extra penny she made as a secretary to pay for this vacation. It had seemed as if she'd thought of everything when she'd mapped out her trip to Wadi el Gemal. She'd decided to spend one week at the national park's Eco-lodge, a tented camp set up in the heart of the park. She would go on guided tours through the desert, and maybe see some of the many sooty falcons that lived there. Getting lost in the middle of said desert had not been on her list of things to do while in Egypt.

Codie hefted her backpack higher up onto her shoulders and turned in a circle, hoping to find some sign of the tour she had been with. A freak sand storm had suddenly blown up, causing her to become separated from the rest of the group. She saw only sandy desert as far as the eye could see. She was in trouble.

"This is so not good."

Starting to panic, she reached up and wrapped her hand around the pendant she wore on her neck.

It had been a gift from her grandmother when she turned thirteen. The pendant was a golden Eye of Horus. The eye in the center held a large turquoise — her birth stone. Codie never took it off. From the moment she had first put it on she'd felt that as long as she wore it, she would be protected. After she'd done some research to find out what the Eye of Horus meant, she hadn't been surprised to learn the ancient Egyptians used it to protect against evil.

With a tight grip on her pendant, some of her panic receded. She forced herself to keep her breathing even. "Calm down, Codie."

Hyperventilating wouldn't make her situation any better. The tour guide would eventually notice her missing. Once he did, a search party would be sent out for her. She couldn't have wandered that far into the desert. At least she hoped she hadn't.

Codie took stock of her situation. She had been wandering on her own for at least an hour before she'd finally admitted she was lost. She found herself out in the open with the sun beating down on her, but at night the temperature would drop, becoming quite cold. There could be a slim chance she wouldn't be rescued before darkness fell. If that happened, she didn't want to be stuck out in the open without any kind of shelter. She did have a sleeping bag with her backpack, but she didn't have a tent. She needed to find some kind of vegetation big enough to shade her from the sun's rays during the day and offer her some kind of shelter at night. That left her only one option — she would have to start looking for such a place.

She would be doing what all the experts said not to do when someone became lost, but she didn't think she had any other option. She rubbed her thumb across the surface of the turquoise and pulled her baseball cap lower on her forehead as she walked.

The day grew hotter. Thankfully, she'd had the foresight to don a light-weight long-sleeved shirt and pants. Having natural auburn hair, she had the fair skin to go along with it. She would have already been burnt to a crisp if she had been in a tank top and shorts. As it stood now, she felt her face slowly getting sunburned.

After another hour of walking, Codie found what she'd been looking for. About sixty feet in front of her stood some kind of tall, shrubby tree that she had no name for. No other vegetation grew around it. It would have to do. She couldn't keep wandering around the desert. She already was thirsty. Luckily, she'd put two large bottles of water into her backpack that morning before she'd set out on the tour. If she rationed herself wisely, she should have enough to last her for a day or so.

Once in the shade of the shrubby tree, Codie took off her backpack and then took out one of the water bottles. She drank the water sparingly. To set up her "camp," she untied her sleeping bag from her pack before she placed it under the tree. She scanned the area, surprised to find a fair amount of deadwood littered on the ground. Having known how cold the desert became at night, she had made sure to bring a lighter with her, even though she didn't smoke. With that and the deadwood, she'd be able to have a fire that night.

Codie collected a pile of wood, which she stacked near her sleeping bag. With her "camp" arranged, she could do nothing else but sit and wait.

The remaining hours of the day slowly ticked by. Whenever she started to panic, Codie reached for her Eye of Horus pendant. With the turquoise nestled in her palm, she sent out a silent prayer that someone would find her. Once night descended, she even sent out a prayer to the Egyptian god, Horus.

Just before it grew completely dark, Codie managed to start a small fire. She would have to wake up every few hours to add more wood to the fire. She crawled into her sleeping bag. The stress of the day had finally taken its toll. Her eyes fluttered shut. Before sleep claimed her, she reached up to stroke the turquoise hanging around her neck. As tired as she felt, she almost didn't notice the heat that radiated off the blue stone and seeped into her fingertips. She gripped the pendant as she drifted off to sleep.

* * * *

It had to be a dream. Codie stared around the luxurious room she found herself in. The walls had been painted in jewel tones with Egyptian hieroglyphs carved into the stone. Off to one side, a huge bed sat on top a platform with sheer drapes surrounding it. A couple smoking braziers gave off the scent of the incense that had been thrown onto the hot coals. She stepped farther into the room and skipped her gaze over the mound of brightly colored pillows thrown on the floor near one of the braziers. Not until she looked at the very back of the room did she draw up short. There sat a large throne-like chair placed upon a raised dais. And on the chair sat a man quietly watching her.

As he stood and slowly walked toward her, Codie could only stare. He was like no other man she had ever encountered before. He looked as if he had stepped out of one of the ancient Egyptian pictures painted on the walls. He wore only a white linen kilt, which left most of his body bared. He was so muscular she could see the muscles bunching under his bronzed skin as he walked. Unable to look away, she dragged her eyes across the wide expanse of his chest and down to his well-defined abs. Her mouth went dry. She always found herself to be attracted to muscular men, the bigger the muscles the more she wanted the man. Just looking at his half-naked body caused her knees to go weak, and she hadn't even had a good look at his face yet.

She pulled her gaze back up his body and looked at his face as he came to stand in front of her. Her breath caught in her lungs. It matched his body. Swallowing hard, she skimmed her gaze over the hard planes and angles of his face. She took him all in and noted his shoulder-length, straight, black hair and dark brown eyes. His firm lips were formed into a half smile. And he appeared to be tall, well over six feet, which was something else she liked in a man. Being five-foot-ten, she rarely found herself in the position of having to look up at a man as she had to do with this one.

Codie licked her dry lips. His gaze drifted down to her mouth and stayed there. "Hi." When her voice broke, she cleared her throat and tried again. "Hi."

"Hello." He spoke in heavily accented English. He dragged his gaze up to her eyes, and asked, "You have need of me?"

Oh, she needed him all right. She'd be more than happy to have him in her bed, taking care of her needs all night long. He chuckled, almost as if he had read her thoughts. Codie tried to pull her mind out of the gutter, but she couldn't completely manage it with that gorgeous male body in front of her. Her fingers itched to touch every inch of him, including what he had under his kilt. As he chuckled again, she forced herself to speak.

"I'm not sure. I know this is a dream, and that I've made this all up in my mind."

"Yes, this is a dream. You called me to you."

"I did? I don't even know who you are." Without thinking about it, Codie reached up to touch her pendant. His gaze followed her movement.

"Yes, you did." He brushed her fingers aside before he

lifted the pendant away from her skin. "You wear my eye. You used the pendant to call me."

"You're Horus? The Egyptian god, Horus?" Now she knew for sure this had to be a figment of her imagination. Her subconscious had created this other place to help her cope with the extreme situation she found herself in.

"I am. And you are?"

"Codie. My name is Codie."

"It has been many years since a mortal has called out to me, intentionally or unintentionally."

"It has?" Codie's heart raced as he took another step closer. There was barely an inch between their bodies now. For a dream, her mind had done a pretty good job of imagining what Horus would look like. It only seemed right that an Egyptian god would have a perfect face and body.

"Since you have called out for me, I assume there is an urgent need for my assistance." Horus suggestively looked her up and down.

Codie's insides turned to jelly. She knew exactly what he referred to — sex. That a man of his caliber could be interested her in *that* way did a lot for her ego. Normally, in real life, guys like Horus wouldn't give her the time of day. Her looks could only be called average, like most things about her. The only thing that made her stand out was her height.

She usually didn't jump into the sack with a man she had met minutes before, but this was her dream, and being such, she could do whatever she wanted with no reprisals. And right now, she found herself more than willing to have Horus take her to bed.

With more daring than the Codie in the real world would have had, she closed the remaining distance between them until the toes of her hiking boots touched his sandaled feet and placed a hand on his hard chest.

"There is one need I think you're more than capable of

satisfying."

Horus placed his large hand on top hers. "More than capable." He leaned forward and gently brushed her lips with his.

Codie closed her eyes and sighed as his mouth returned to take full possession of hers. At first, his firm lips gently moved over hers. His became more demanding only when she returned his kiss.

He licked along the seam of her mouth, and Codie parted her lips for him. His tongue dueled with hers before he sucked hers into his mouth. She moaned. At the sound, Horus released her hand and wrapped his arms around her waist, pulling her up against his muscled body. The hard length of his cock pressed against her belly. She clutched his shoulders and pressed even closer as an ache built between her legs. Her pussy grew wet in anticipation of what was to come.

Horus left her mouth and trailed his lips along her jaw, down to the side of her neck. He licked and kissed his way to the hollow of her throat. He held her tight against him, bent slightly over his arm, giving himself better access to her breasts. He tongued her nipples through the material of her shirt. They pebbled, and her breasts grew heavy. A gasp escaped her lips when Horus took a nipple between his teeth and gently tugged.

Even though Horus had fanned the flames of her desire ever higher, a sudden chill swept through Codie. She pulled him back up to her mouth as she pressed closer so their bodies touched from chest to thigh. The heat of his body soaked into hers, but it did nothing to stop her from shivering with cold. She moaned, but not with desire. She felt too cold. She shivered uncontrollably.

Horus pulled away to look at her. "What is the matter?'

"Cold. So very cold."

Even as she said the words, Codie felt herself slipping away from this dream world. Knowing she was going to wake up alone, lost in the desert, she let the fear she felt show in her eyes. Horus' brows drew together in concern. She desperately wanted to stay with him. She tried to keep her hold on him, but her fingers lost their solidity. With a whimper of anguish, the room fell away, leaving nothing but darkness surrounding her.

CHAPTER TWO

Racked with chills, Codie woke up with a start. The harsh reality of being lost and alone crashed in on her. Being held in Horus' warm arms one minute, even if it had been a dream, and then thrust back to her present circumstances, made what she had to endure that much worse.

Codie sat up in her sleeping bag and clenched her jaw so her teeth wouldn't chatter from the cold.

"Well, crap," she said.

She peered at the small fire she had started before lying down to sleep. Only a few coals remained. Codie dragged herself out of her sleeping bag, and with fingers stiff from the cold, clumsily pushed some small twigs she had gathered earlier into the hot embers. Gently, she blew on them, forcing the bits of wood to ignite. Once flames greedily licked at them, she placed some larger pieces onto the fire.

Now that she had it going again, she held her hands over its welcoming heat. She looked up at the sky. From the lightening of the sky, it had to be almost dawn. Somehow she had managed to survive her first night out in the desert.

Codie dared to sit as close as she could to the fire before she pulled a water bottle out of her backpack. She drained what remained from the day before. That left her with only one remaining. If a search party didn't find her today, she would be in dire straits. Without water, her chances of survival would be next to nil.

* * * *

Horus dropped his arms to his sides now that he no longer held Codie. Her vanishing meant she had left her dreams and had returned to the mortal realm, much to his disappointment. His cock throbbed beneath his kilt. Never before had a mortal woman aroused him so quickly, or so strongly.

Focusing intently inside himself, he searched the mortal realm for Codie. Something had to wrong. She may not have known what she had done when she had called out to him for help, but her doing so had not been done on a mere whim. The fear he had seen in her eyes before she had vanished had been all too real.

That she wore his turquoise eye around her neck made it easier to find her. He homed in on the stone, getting a clear picture of Codie inside his mind. He stiffened as he took in her surroundings. Connected to her through the stone, he felt the fear she wouldn't allow to take hold of her. Horus touched her thoughts. She was lost out in the desert, alone, with no food and a minimal amount of water. Since she hadn't allowed herself to panic, it spoke volumes of her inner strength.

He wanted to go to her, but he knew he couldn't. If he appeared to her in the mortal realm, it would only draw the unwanted attention of his uncle. He and Seth had become enemies the day his uncle had killed and dismembered his father, Osiris. To this day they remained as adversaries, having fought a number of battles over the centuries. If Horus showed any sign of interest in Codie, in any way, Seth would try to use her against him.

As the sun slowly climbed higher, Horus tried to will Codie to sleep, the only time he could come to her, but she refused to give in. He easily read her worry she. She worried if she slept, those who would come looking for her would miss seeing her.

By the time the sun rose to its hottest, Horus could no longer stand by and watch helplessly as Codie suffered. There had to be something special about this mortal woman that made him want to protect her as if she belonged to him. Using the only option open to him, Horus embraced the falcon in him.

* * * *

The day continued to torment her. The heat coming off the sand rolled over Codie in hot waves, sucking all the moisture out of her. Dying of thirst, she wouldn't allow herself to drink the amount of water she would need to quench it. The few sips she had taken had been barely enough to wet her tongue.

Codie shaded her eyes with her hand and scanned the endless sea of sand. "Where can they be?"

She couldn't understand why no one came for her. They surely had to have noticed her missing by now. She couldn't shake the feeling that someone, or something, purposely kept her out there in the desert.

She closed her eyes, wanting nothing more than to lie back down in her sleeping bag and fall sleep. She fought the urge. She needed to stay awake, to keep looking for any signs of a rescue party. She now knew why the local tribes did nothing during the hottest part of the day. The heat became almost unbearable. Just breathing felt like a chore. The heat—so intense it felt as if a heavy weight sat on her chest—didn't allow her to take a deep breath.

The cries of a falcon had Codie searching the sky, trying to catch a glimpse of it. Once she spotted it, she watched in surprised as it set a course toward her. It circled above her twice before it landed on one of the branches of the tree she sat under. She craned her neck to look up at it.

It was a sooty falcon. A population of them could be found on Wadi El Gemal Island, so seeing one at the national park wouldn't be much of a surprise. What really surprised her was seeing one so far out in the desert. The falcons usually kept to the rocky coast of the Red Sea.

The falcon hopped to the end of the branch it had perched on and then stared back at her. From its size, Codie guessed it to be a male of the species. The females were larger than the males. She smiled up at it, welcome for that small distraction.

"Hello, there."

The falcon let out another cry, then jumped off the branch to land on the ground at her feet.

Codie blinked in surprise. This had to be a wild falcon. It should have wanted to move farther away from her, not get closer. Slowly, to avoid startling it, she pulled her legs up and under her. She kept an eye on his sharp beak and talons. She didn't want to be on the receiving end of either of those. They could quite easily rip her skin to shreds.

Unbelievably, the falcon hopped even closer. He came so close Codie could reach out and stroke the slate-gray feathers covering his chest. As that thought came to mind, she had the urge to do just that. She licked her dry, cracked lips and cautiously held out her hand. Before her fingers made contact, the falcon hopped onto her outstretched arm.

Stunned, Codie froze. She had a wild falcon using her as a perch. She waited for his talons to dig into her wrist, but the falcon only lightly gripped her. Her arm soon grew tired of being held out for so long. Smoothly as she could manage, she pulled it back up against her side with her forearm still held out. The falcon stayed where he perched, unperturbed by the movement.

Codie shook her head and smiled. "Have you come to keep me company, or are you as lost in the desert as I am?" The falcon shifted on her arm and turned his head to stare at her. "You're obviously not afraid of humans. I wonder why."

She looked into the falcon's eyes and thought she saw intelligence lurking in their depths. She shook her head. The heat must be getting to her if she thought the falcon had understood what she had said. She wished he could. How much easier it would be to be able to tell him to get help for her, instead of sitting there waiting it to come to her.

As the minutes ticked by and the falcon didn't seem to have any interest in leaving, Codie decided he was more than welcome to stay with her. She reached for her backpack one handed with the intention of having some water. She managed to unzip it and take out the bottle, but with the falcon sitting on her arm it made it difficult for her to get the lid off. She shifted once again so that she sat on her bottom, held the bottle between her legs and twisted off the cap.

After taking a few small sips, she held the bottle up to see how much water remained. She had drunk over half. Codie turned to look at the falcon. It appeared as if he too peered at the water.

She shook her head. "Sorry, my friend, but that's all I have. I can't give you any of it. There's barely enough there for me as it is. If you're thirsty, you'll have to find some for yourself. Same goes for food. I haven't had anything to eat since early yesterday."

The falcon let out a cry before he launched himself into the air. Startled by his sudden leave-taking, Codie just about jumped out of her skin. The falcon flew off until it appeared to be nothing more than a small speak in the sky.

"Was it something I said?" she called after him.

The day grew later, and Codie resigned herself to spending another night out in the desert. She gathered some more of the wood around her and prepared it to light once darkness fell. Her stomach rumbled, protesting the lack of food. She didn't know if she could survive another day out in the baking sun with no food and little to no water. It would be a matter of time before she broke down mentally. If only the falcon would come back. She hadn't felt so alone with him near her.

* * * *

Horus soared through the air, quickly winging his way to the Red Sea coast. Codie's plight could only be described as dire. She needed food and water if she hoped to survive many more days out in the desert. As an Egyptian god, he didn't need neither food nor water, but mortals needed both to sustain their lives.

Seeing the sparkling water of the sea ahead of him, Horus increased his speed. He flew over it to a spot where it'd be very deep. He hovered and used his powers to call a fish to the surface. A true falcon didn't catch fish. They mostly ate insects and lizards, but he didn't think Codie would eat any of those things, no matter how hungry she became.

It didn't take long for a large fish to answer his summons. As it came to the surface, he snatched it out of the water with his sharp talons. He flapped his strong wings, rose into the air and used his sharp beak to kill the fish.

Darkness had slowly descended once he reached Codie's small camp. She sat before the fire she'd built, staring forlornly at the flames. At his cry, she looked up and smiled brightly. He circled her once before he flew close to the fire and threw the fish into the hot coals at the very edge of it. Satisfied that she would easily be able to retrieve it after it cooked, Horus carefully landed on her shoulder. She tentatively reached up and stroked his chest.

"You came back, and you brought me a present as well. I'm beginning to think you're no ordinary falcon."

Horus rubbed his feathered head against her ear. For now, he would let her believe he was one of the many wild falcons in the area. After the fish had sat long enough in the coals to be fully cooked, Codie dragged it out and then hungrily pull it apart with her fingers to get at the meat. As she ate, he sent out his senses. There had to be something not right about this whole situation. This area belonged to the national park. There should have been other mortals around, at the very least some of the local tribes should have been nearby, but there appeared to be no one else. He searched deeper and stiffened. His senses picked up something that shouldn't have been there.

Something invisible, like a shield, surrounded Codie and her camp. It was enough to physically stop others from coming near her, and for her to be overlooked, as if she really wasn't there. He picked up on a spell that had been added to the barrier, one that would make anything or anyone coming near it turn away before they came too close. The whole thing reeked of his uncle's handiwork. Seth had, for some reason, singled Codie out. Why he had done so, Horus could not say.

After Codie finished her meal, Horus hopped off her shoulder and fluttered to the ground. She placed more wood on the fire before she climbed into her sleeping bag. Once she fell into a deep sleep, he closed his eyes and joined her in her dream.

CHAPTER THREE

She found herself back in the room she had dreamed of the night before. Everything about it appeared to be exactly the same, even down to having the god Horus, who stood near the large platform bed seemingly waiting for her. Codie reached up and touched her pendant. He had said the last time that she had called him by using his eye. She didn't think she had done so at this moment. She had hoped she would see him in her dreams again just before sleep claimed her. That could be one reason she found herself there once again.

Horus reached out to her. "Codie, come to me."

The sound of his deep, accented voice saying her name sent shivers of awareness through her. Codie crossed the distance between them and then slipped her hand into his. Horus pulled her close, holding her tightly against him. She closed her eyes, savoring the feel of just being held. She needed this more than anything—the contact, the feel of someone wanting to hold her protectively.

He soon released her and pushed her to sit on the bed. Horus set to work removing her hiking boots and socks. Once he pulled her to her feet again, he slowly stripped off her shirt and pants. His gaze greedily took in the sight of her only in her bra and panties. After he stepped away and went to one of the smoking braziers, Codie wondered what he could be up to.

He picked up a large bowl. He soon returned to the bed and then placed what he carried onto the floor at their feet. Codie realized what Horus intended to do when she saw the steaming water. A lotus bloom floated on its surface, filling the air with its scent. Horus plucked out the cloth that had been soaking in the water and wrung it out. Turning to her, he gently ran it against her face.

Codie's body flared to life. She found the simple task of this man, this god, washing her face, to be highly erotic. Her pulse quickened as he slowly moved the cloth down her throat to her chest. He dipped the cloth back into the bowl and then wrung it out before swiping it across her upper chest. He seemed to falter when he encountered her bra. She had a feeling he wanted to remove it, but didn't have any idea how to go about it. She took matters into her own hands. She reached behind her, quickly unhooked her bra and let it drop to the floor.

Horus wiped the wet cloth over her breasts. Her nipples tightened into buds, begging for attention. Codie wanted to feel his mouth on her skin, but he frustratingly continued to touch her only with the cloth.

He thoroughly washed each of her arms before he once again focused his attention back to her breasts. Codie took her bottom lip between her teeth as Horus bent and swirled his tongue around each tight peak. She tried to press closer, but he didn't allow it.

"Let me do this first for you, Codie. It will make you feel better. Lie down on the bed."

Codie did as he asked. Horus dipped the cloth back into the bowl before he continued to wash her. It did feel good, but she wanted more. As the cloth moved across her ribcage and down to her stomach, she clutched the sheets beneath her. Goose bumps broke out along her skin as Horus blew across her damp flesh.

At her hips, Horus shifted the cloth to wipe one of her legs. Codie barely suppressed a groan of frustration. He looked up at her and smiled knowingly before turning back to run the cloth over her other leg. Once he finished with her legs, he urged her over onto her stomach.

He pushed her hair aside before he washed her back and the backs of her legs. At the feel of the cloth being run along the inside of her thighs, Codie held her breath, waiting for Horus to touch her in the most intimate of places. She gasped as his knuckles brushed against her hot opening.

Horus dropped the cloth into the bowl and had Codie turn over onto her back. He stared down at her with longing in his eyes. She reached up, wrapped her hand around the back of his neck and pulled him to her.

Aroused from his ministrations with the cloth, Codie pressed her lips to his. She slanted her mouth over his and kissed him deeply. Still kissing her, Horus shifted until he lay on his side next to her. She moaned as one of his large hands covered her breast.

Horus increased the pressure of his lips and used his tongue to urge her to open for him. She parted her lips and placed her hands onto his wide shoulders, holding him close. He stroked the inside of her mouth, thoroughly tasting her. In response, her pussy pulsed with need.

He dragged his lips from hers and trailed them down along her jaw to her throat. As he pressed against her, the hard length of his cock snuggled against her hip. He continued downward. He cupped her breast and lifted it to his mouth. With the tip of his tongue, he flicked it a couple times against her nipple before he sucked it deep inside. Codie moaned again.

Horus moved to her other breast as he stroked his hand down across her flat stomach. He pushed it under the waistband of her panties, then delved deeper. He stroked her clit before he pushed a finger slowly into her wet opening. Codie arched her hips, squeezing down on the digit, and rode it as he moved it in and out of her.

He claimed her lips in a searing kiss as he removed his finger, took hold of the top of her panties and pulled them all the way off. Codie could no longer hold herself back from touching him. She shifted so she lay on her side before she reached between them and stroked his cock through the material of his kilt. It jumped beneath her fingers.

Horus lifted himself slightly away from her as he made short work of removing his kilt and the loincloth he wore beneath it. Now completely naked as she, he took her hand and led it to his fully erect cock. He groaned as Codie wrapped her fingers around his thick shaft and squeezed.

Codie stroked her hand up and down him, moaning at the thought of how good it would feel to have his hard length buried deep inside her. Wetness pooled between her legs. She ached to have him possess her.

Horus soon pulled her hand away and then rolled her onto her back. He released her mouth and slid down the length of her body, placing kisses across her stomach and hips as he went. He used his upper body to spread her legs farther apart, exposing her slick opening to his view. He cupped her bottom, lifted her to him and licked her pussy with the flat of his tongue.

Codie let her eyes fall shut as he licked and sucked. Moaning, she rocked her hips into him as he alternated between flicking her clit with his tongue and sucking on it. Not until he pushed two fingers inside her, moving them in and out as he sucked on her clit, did Codie feel the pressure build inside her. She couldn't take much more of this without climaxing, but she didn't want to come this way. She wanted him inside her when she found her release.

She yanked on Horus' hair and pulled him back up her body. Codie threaded her fingers through his black hair as she kissed him passionately. With her free hand, she took hold of his hard cock and led it to the opening of her body. He rubbed the head of it against her, coating himself with her juices. Then inch by slow inch, he pushed inside her. They both moaned once he had completely sheathed himself to the hilt.

Codie luxuriated in the feel of him stretching her, filling her to capacity. It felt so good. He moved inside her, and she forgot to breath. She pressed the flat of her feet onto the mattress and matched his strokes. He pumped into her slowly at first, until he had her clawing his back.

Increasing his pace, Horus placed his hands beneath her and angled her hips so his hard shaft rubbed her clit with each stroke. Codie clutched him as she squeezed her inner muscles around him. Her release inched ever closer.

Horus rode her faster, and his cock grow even harder. She whimpered as her release crashed through her. Horus continued to move inside her as her body rhythmically squeezed his thick length. Once her body started to come back down to earth, he pumped his hips into her twice before he found his own release. His shaft pulsed deep inside her, filling her with his cum.

He kept their bodies joined as he rolled them to their sides. He pulled Codie close and kissed her sweaty forehead. "You are mine now."

Codie snuggled close, but now that they were no longer making love, a chill came over her. Not wanting to leave Horus, she looked up at him. "I feel the cold. The fire must be out. I don't want this dream to end. What if I can't come back?"

Horus stroked the side of her face. "You will come back to me." He placed his hand on the turquoise eye she wore around her neck. "As long as you wear this, I can find you. Don't fear, Codie. You aren't alone. Whenever you sleep,

I'll be here waiting for you."

She felt herself slipping away. She quickly pressed her lips to his, hoping that what Horus said wouldn't turn out to be untrue. That she could return to him whenever she slept. He had become her lifeline now. If she lost him, she didn't know what she would do.

* * * *

After Codie disappeared, Horus let out a groan of frustration. He wanted her still. The one time had not satisfied his longing for her. He wanted her there, lying in the bed next to him as she pressed her naked body to his. He still tasted her on his tongue, and smelled her scent on him. Yes, his turquoise eye tied them together, but it was much more than that. She completed him. Making love to her had proved how right it felt to have her in his arms, their bodies joined as one.

Horus quickly rolled off the bed. It didn't take him long to don his loin cloth and kilt. He needed to return to Codie in his falcon form. If Seth did have plans for her, he didn't want her to be alone. He had claimed her as his. He couldn't allow his uncle to have her.

CHAPTER FOUR

odie drank what remained of her water. It hadn't been enough. She was getting severely dehydrated. Her tongue felt thick and her lips had cracked. She could barely work up enough saliva to swallow.

She placed the empty water bottle back into her pack and then lay down on her sleeping bag. She had given up hope of ever being found. She briefly thought of trying to find her own way out of the desert, but quickly decided against it. With no water, being out in the open would be a sure way to die. Besides that, she was too weak to even try. The lack of water had made her lethargic.

She scanned the skies. The falcon had been gone when she had awakened. She'd had to fight back the tears that threatened to spill over when she noticed he had left her. Crying over a bird would not do her any good. Nor would losing what moisture she had left in her body by shedding useless tears.

Codie closed her eyes and held on to her pendant. She wanted to sleep, to return to her dream lover, but it eluded her. Instead, she whispered Horus' name, wishing he was as real as the Horus she had made love to while asleep. If he were a real god and not part of her delusional fantasy, he certainly would have been able to get her out of the desert.

The cry of a falcon had her quickly trying to sit up. Not wanting to get her hopes up that it would be her falcon, as she had come to think of him, Codie shaded her eyes and watched a dark spot come ever closer. Seeing that it indeed appeared to be the same falcon, and that he had brought her another fish, she squashed the tears of relief that burned behind her eyes.

The falcon swooped in and dropped the fish so it landed on the ground next to her. He circled back and came to land close to where she sat. Codie reached out and smiled as he hopped up onto her arm.

With the back of her hand, she stroked the feathers on his chest. "So that's where you've been. You went fishing for me again." Almost as if he understood her, the falcon bobbed his head. Codie smiled.

After turning to look at the large fish, she debated whether or not to relight the fire. She didn't like to eat sushi, but with her wood supply so low, she really didn't have much choice in the matter. She'd been snapping off branches of the tree that she used for shelter. She couldn't afford to lose its shade.

With a gulp, Codie brought the fish closer. Luckily for her, the falcon had already killed it. She reached into her pack and then pulled out the multi-tool she had brought with her. After watching a few survival type shows, and seeing how it had helped the survivors in many ways, she'd picked one up. Also from watching one of those shows she'd learned that eating raw fish helped replace some of the moisture in one's body. It seemed all well and good to know that information, but actually having to eat the raw fish would be another matter entirely.

Codie flipped open the knife in the multi-tool before she slowly cut a slit down the fish's belly. As she worked, the falcon perched on her shoulder. She tried not to gag as she pulled out the guts. She threw them away from her, to be buried in the sand as she had done with the remnants of the fish from the day before. Once she cut one side of the fish off, she sliced a small section away. Before she could really think about what she'd be eating, she popped the raw fish into her mouth and chewed as quickly as she could. It took her a couple tries to get it all down, but at least it stayed there.

She managed to just about finish a quarter of the fish before her stomach rebelled. Not wanting to throw up the much needed nourishment, Codie set it aside. She didn't know what to do with the rest. Thinking maybe the falcon would eat what remained, she cut a piece from it and offered it to the bird. Not interested in the food, he turned his head away.

With a shrug, she said, "At least you can afford to be picky."

Codie set about clearing away the mess. Once finished, she used sand and charcoal to clean the fish from her hands. The falcon screamed, hopped off her shoulder and suddenly took to the air. Wondering what had upset him, she looked in the direction the falcon had flown. In the distance, what looked like a brown wave was headed in her direction. It took a few minutes for her brain to process what she looked at. Another sand storm had moved in.

The falcon dive bombed her, pushing her back toward her sleeping bag. Realizing it would be the only cover available, Codie quickly got into it and then zipped it around her. She scrunched down until it covered her head before she pulled the ends in. The falcon cried again seconds before the sand storm hit. Lying, listening to the wind howling around her, she hoped he'd managed to fly away in time.

Codie lost all track of time. She had no idea how long the stand storm lasted. After the wind finally subsided and she no longer felt the sand buffeting her, she slowly pulled the sleeping bag away from her head. The sight that met her eyes made her want to cry. The sand had torn through her camp, obliterating everything in its path. The tree, her only respite from the sun's burning rays, had taken a lot of damage. Most of its branches had been ripped away, leaving her exposed.

Disheartened, Codie pulled the sleeping bag back over her head. Defeated, she touched the turquoise around her neck and willed herself to sleep.

* * * *

Horus sensed the instant Codie fell asleep. In mid-flight, he willed himself to her. She stood in the middle of his chamber, looking lost and forlorn. The sand storm had taken its toll on her. His temper flared. He fisted his hands at his sides. As soon as the storm had hit, he'd known it'd been his uncle's handiwork. Somehow Seth must have realized Horus had come to help her in his falcon form. He quickly pushed back his anger as she turned to face him. At the sight of a lone tear streaking down her cheek, he held open his arms. She quickly crossed the distance between them and threw herself at him.

She held him tightly, almost as if she were afraid to let him go. "I can't do this anymore, Horus. It's too much. I don't want to ever wake up."

Horus took her by the arms and pulled Codie away from him so he could look into her eyes. "Don't say that. You must not give up hope. You will survive this."

"How can I? It's all gone. I don't have any more water. The sand storm took away the only shade I had. I'm going to roast out in the sun. Please. I just want to stay here with you."

Horus felt Codie slipping away. Not back to the mortal realm, but to the place that would only lead to her death.

Knowing of one way to keep her there with him, he pulled her up against him and claimed her lips in a searing kiss. He poured all that he felt for her into it. He could easily lose her, and he never wanted to let her go. He loved her as he had never loved anything in his very long life. She made him feel things he'd never felt before. She would survive this, and once she returned to safety, he'd come to her and claim her as his mate in the real world.

He scooped her up into his arms and then carried her to the bed. He placed her onto it, then followed her down so he lay half on top her. Continuing to kiss her, he urged her lips apart, needing to taste her. She moaned into his mouth, telling as nothing else would that she had completely returned to him.

Not having the patience to do it the mortal way, Horus willed their clothes away. The feel of her naked skin pressed to him sent his senses reeling. He cupped her full breast, left her mouth and flicked his tongue against her taut nipple. Codie moaned again as she clutched his shoulders. He tongued her nipple again and then sucked it deep inside his mouth. She threaded her fingers through his hair, holding him to her as he sucked at her breast.

Horus released her nipple before he dragged his tongue up her chest to her chin, nipping it with his teeth. "Touch me, Codie. I need to feel your hands on my body."

Codie traced a finger along his lips. "I want to touch you. Just the thought of having you on your back, letting me have my way with you turns me on like nothing else. I didn't get a chance the last time."

His cock jumped at the thought of having Codie on top him as she ran her mouth and tongue over every inch of his body. He rolled onto his back and pulled her so she lay sprawled atop him.

"Now's your chance to torture me with that sweet-tasting mouth of yours."

A small smile played on Codie's lips. "Oh, I intend to

do just that."

She sat up so she straddled his hips and then traced the muscles of his chest with heavy lidded eyes. She had thrown her long auburn hair over her shoulders, giving him an unobstructed view of her full breasts. He circled her rose-hued nipples with the tip of his finger. Codie pushed his hand away.

"You're not going to distract me. I haven't even begun yet."

Codie leaned forward and placed small kisses across the width of his chest. Once she reached his nipples, she dragged the flat of her tongue across them. With maddening slowness, she inched down on his body. She pressed her lips to his skin, flicking her tongue against it. The lower she went the more his cock throbbed.

At the first touch of her fingers on his hard cock, Horus groaned. It felt like torture. He resisted the urge to flip Codie onto her back and thrust into her welcoming heat. He could tell she enjoyed what she did to him. He didn't want to take that pleasure away from her.

Gently, she dragged her nails up his full length. At the tip, she used her finger to rub the bead of moisture she found there into his skin. She licked her lips, took a firm hold of his cock and bent to circle the head with her tongue. Horus moaned. The feel of her mouth on him, pleasuring him, almost became too much. The feeling increased when Codie opened her mouth and took as much of his cock into her mouth as she could manage. He flexed his hips as she alternated between sucking and swirling her tongue around the head of his shaft.

Just before he reached the point of no return, Horus tugged on Codie's arm. She released him and shifted so his cock nestled against her dripping pussy. She shifted again and positioned herself. Once she had him where she wanted him, she slowly pushed down, impaling herself on his hard shaft.

With her bottom lip between her teeth, Codie sat up and slowly rode him. After finding her pace, she arched her hips as she slid up and down his thick shaft. In this position, he was buried so deeply inside her the head of his cock hit her cervix with each stroke in. Her strong inner muscles clutched around him, squeezing him. Her breasts bounced slightly as she moved on him.

Horus' climax built, but he wanted Codie to come first. He placed a finger where their two bodies joined and rubbed her clit. Her movements grew jerky. Soon a keening moan slipped past her lips as her orgasm took her over. With her body clutching his, he could no longer hold back his release. He firmly held on to her hips as he thrust into her. As an intense orgasm tore through him, he arched up into her, almost lifting her off the bed.

Codie collapsed on top him. Horus wrapped his arms around her, holding her close. Slowly their breathing returned to normal. He gently pushed her hair away from her face. She turned her head and placed a kiss onto his chest. She propped her chin on it so she could look up at him.

"I don't want to go back, Horus. It feels too good to be here like this with you."

"I'd like nothing more than for you to stay with me, Codie, but you must return. You're my mate. I won't give you up without a fight. I won't allow death to take you from me."

"I want to be your mate, but no one has found me, and my time is running out. Why haven't they found me?"

Before Horus could answer her, he stiffened beneath her. Something was wrong. He sucked in a breath as an image flashed inside his mind.

He took Codie's face between his hands and stared into her eyes. "You have to wake up now, Codie. When you do, don't move until I come to you. Do you understand?"

Codie nodded. Horus hoped she'd do as he'd asked as

he gave her a mental push that would send her back to her body and wakefulness.

CHAPTER FIVE

Suddenly awake, Codie found herself back in the stifling confines of her sleeping bag. Drenched in sweat, she felt as if she couldn't get enough oxygen. Even though in her dream Horus had told her not to move, she needed air. Not really knowing why he would have wanted her to remain still, she slowly pushed her head out. The instant her it cleared the top of the bag, she froze.

Not a foot away from where she lay sat a sand viper, coiled, ready to strike. Codie took shallow breaths so as not to cause the viper to strike and stared at it in horror. It was one of the most poisonous snakes in Egypt. One bite from it would be enough to kill.

The viper's tongue flicked in and out, scenting the air. Her muscles clenched from the effort it took not to move. Her brain screamed at her to run, but that would be the worst thing to do. Horus had said to wait for him to come to her before he had sent her back. Realistically, Codie didn't think she had a chance in hell of having a real Egyptian god come to her rescue. She only hoped if she stayed still long enough the viper would lose interest in her and be on its way.

As the viper coiled its body tighter, Codie knew her luck had run out. Just as she expected it to strike, her falcon swooped down and snatched it up in his sharp talons. He dropped to the sand a short distance away and jabbed his sharp beak through the snake's head, killing it instantly.

Codie unzipped her sleeping bag and then sat up. The falcon picked the dead snake up in its beak and threw it away. He hopped toward her. He'd swooped out of the sky, honing directly on the snake. She realized this couldn't be an ordinary falcon.

It couldn't be a coincidence that she wore the Eye of Horus around her neck, and that a falcon had come to her in her time of need. Nor the fact that every time she slept she had dreams of him, and erotic ones at that. In ancient Egyptian art Horus was represented as a falcon-headed god, or just as a falcon. Could this one really be *the* Horus?

Codie studied the falcon as he hopped up onto her outstretched arm. "Horus?" she whispered.

The falcon cocked his head to the side and stared back at her. Codie shook her head at her foolishness. This had to be a wild sooty falcon, one, for some reason, had attached himself to her. He probably sensed she needed help. Wild dolphins had been documented helping survivors whose ships had sunk in the ocean. And reportedly, some of those dolphins had even managed to drive away sharks before they could attack the people they protected. The falcon had to have done the same thing for her when he'd killed the sand viper.

The day wore on. Her thirst grew more intense as the hours ticked by. Without the tree's shade, the heat felt that much worse. Her baseball cap did little to block the sun's rays. Codie wanted nothing more than to lie back and go to sleep, but each time she tried to do just that, the falcon would scream in warning. The first time he did it, she thought another sand viper had once again found her.

She'd frantically searched the camp, only to realize there was nothing there. The third time she'd tried to sleep, he screamed the instant her head hit her sleeping bag. It dawned on her that he did it on purpose to keep her awake.

By late afternoon, Codie felt really ill. She had to be near to having sun stroke, if she didn't already have it. Even though it was extremely hot, she was racked with chills. She found it hard to think straight.

The falcon had at one point moved off her arm and sat on the sleeping bag next to her. Not once had he left her side, not even when the sun burned at its hottest and he could have gone to find some respite from the heat.

Unable to focus her thoughts in her muddled brain, Codie's head bobbed as she grew more lethargic. The falcon screamed. This time when she looked over at him to tell him he annoyed her each time he did that, she surprisingly found him not looking at her but at something in the distance. She tried to focus her eyes and searched the sand to see what had caught his attention.

At first, she couldn't see anything. Slowly, she focused her eyes on what looked like a small funnel of whirling sand. Shading her eyes to get an even better look, she didn't think it could be another sand storm brewing. It seemed too small and too compact. It came ever closer.

"Oh, shit."

The falcon hopped off the sleeping bag and positioned himself in front of her at her feet.

Once the swirling funnel of sand arrived, it stopped in the middle of her camp. Unbelievably, it stayed in one spot as it hovered a few inches above the ground. The falcon spread his wings, almost as if he wanted to hold the funnel back and wouldn't allow it to come near her. In reaction, the sand funnel changed. It grew taller as the sand slowly dropped to the ground. The shape of a man began to appear inside the swirling sand. Codie rubbed her eyes, thinking they had to be playing a trick on her. The longer she looked, the more the man took shape, taking on solidity bit by bit until he stood tall and strong before her.

Codie stared. The man looked like an ancient Egyptian, dressed in a similar fashion as Horus had been in her dreams. He wore nothing but a pristine white linen kilt. She ran her gaze up his body and noted he was just as muscular as Horus. At his face the similarities ended. He'd be considered good looking, but he had a cruel look about him. His dark brown eyes stared down at her. He had to be able to see how much of a dire situation she found herself in, but from his satisfied smile, she could tell it thrilled him to see her in such a condition.

She jumped as he threw back his head and laughed. He stared down at the falcon. "Well, well, isn't this a nice surprise. Actually, it isn't that much of a surprise. I knew when I first saw her, and saw that she wore your eye around her neck, that you wouldn't be able to resist her. This has worked out far better than I thought it would. How has it felt to watch the one you have sought to protect slowly waste away and not be able to do anything to save her, Horus? I know I've enjoyed watching your pathetic attempts to keep her alive."

Codie sucked in a breath. He had called her falcon Horus. She so very much wanted it to be the truth. She held her breath as the falcon's image wavered. In a matter of seconds, the Horus from her dreams took the falcon's place. He stood with his back to her as he faced down the other man.

"I won't allow you to harm her, Seth. She is mine."

Codie's mind reeled. *Horus was real?* Even though her mind had a hard time accepting that he was, she couldn't discount the fact that he stood in front of her, or the fact that his uncle, Seth, stood there as well. Then again, it could all be a hallucination.

"You've claimed a mortal as your mate? Hmm, that

changes a few of the plans I had for the woman. I think now instead of ending her pathetic life, I'll take her from you."

"That, I will never allow." Out of thin air, a sword appeared in Horus' hand. "You won't win this time."

Seth smiled as a sword similar to the one Horus held, appeared in his. "We shall see who the victor is, Horus."

Codie scooted away from the two men as their swords clanged together. They moved with lethal grace, both intent on doing the most damage to the other. Forgotten, she could only watch silently and hope Horus became the winner. If she ended up in Seth's clutches, she had a feeling things would be far worse for her than what she'd been dealing with for the last few days.

The men parried and thrust. The sounds of their clashing swords filled the air. They seemed to be equally matched in strength and skill. When it seemed neither one would gain the upper hand, Horus blocked Seth's sword and rammed his body into his uncle. Horus grappled Seth to the ground, pinning him there as he held the tip of his sword against Seth's throat.

"Surrender. It's over, Seth. Remove the spell you placed around Codie that has kept her trapped here." Horus growled. "Now this can work either of two ways. You can remove the spell now or I can take your head, ensuring Codie's safety." He moved the tip of his sword to one of Seth's eyes. "Or better yet, I can return the favor and take your eye as you took mine."

Codie held her breath. She knew exactly what Horus meant by returning the favor. According to ancient Egyptian myth, Seth had killed and dismembered Horus' father, Osiris, wanting to claim the Egyptian throne for his own. Wanting revenge, Horus had challenged his uncle to a fight. During the ensuing battle, Seth tore out one of Horus' eyes. After the fight, Thot, the moon god, returned and healed it. The symbol of the Eye of Horus came to be after Horus had lost his.

Seth snarled at his nephew. "You win this time. I've removed the spell, but let's see if you can still save your mate."

Seth waved a hand in Codie's direction. Pain tore through her body. The chills that racked her body increased tenfold. Dizziness assailed her. No longer able to remain upright, she sank onto her sleeping bag. Before darkness rose to claim her, she reached out to Horus and whispered his name.

* * * *

Horus quickly spun around to look at Codie. The moment he removed his attention from his uncle, Seth disappeared. Horus quickly checked to make sure Seth had indeed removed his spell as he rushed to Codie's side. Thankfully, he could no longer detect it.

He lifted Codie into his arms. She shook uncontrollably. He also felt her life slipping away. Horus sent his senses out and searched until he found the rescue party that had been looking for her since she'd become separated from her tour group. He sent them a mental push to come as quickly as they could.

Once the rescuers were almost upon them, Horus laid Codie down onto the sleeping bag. He didn't want to leave her there, but he wanted her to return to her old life before he took the final step that would well and truly make her his mate. He had to allow her to make the final decision of her own free will.

Horus placed a kiss on Codie's fevered brow and quietly promised he would return to her very soon. He disappeared as the rescue party came into sight in the distance.

CHAPTER SIX

Codie woke up a day later in a hospital bed. She didn't feel completely like her old self, but it would only be a matter of time before she did now that she'd been taken out of the desert. The doctor had told her she'd been lucky. If the search party hadn't found her when they had, she would have been dead in a matter of hours.

She really didn't remember much about being found. Her memory of it blurred together. They'd barely managed to rouse her enough to get some much needed water into her before they'd headed out of the desert. That was about all she could recall.

Now awake and hooked up to an IV, slowly her strength returned. And with it came uncertainties. Her dreams had seemed so real, as had seeing Horus coming to defend her that last day she'd been lost. She so much wanted to believe it hadn't all been a product of her imagination. She didn't want to think she'd fallen in love with a man her brain had made up. She had to admit that near the end there, with her body failing and racked with fever, she could have been hallucinating when the battle between Horus and Seth took place.

She didn't want to face reality, to discover Horus didn't exist. Codie debated whether or not to try using her pendant to call him as she'd supposedly done when she'd first seen him. In the end, she couldn't take the not knowing.

Codie waited until she was alone in her hospital room, then clutched her turquoise Eye of Horus pendant in her hand and closed her eyes. She focused her mind on the image of the Horus, who'd walked into her dreams, as she called out to him. Nothing happened. The turquoise stone in the middle of the eye remained cool. That was it then. It hadn't been real. Feeling as if she'd just lost the only man she'd ever love, she swiped at the lone tear that slid down her cheek.

Two days later, the doctor informed her she'd fully recovered and could go home. Codie was happy to be released from the hospital, but she couldn't return to the national park. One of the staff had kindly packed up her belongings and had brought them to her, so she really had no reason to return there.

Before she left the hospital, Codie phoned the airport. She still had one more day left before she had to catch her flight home to Canada, but she wanted to leave now. Surprisingly, she found it an easy task to have her flight changed to one that left later that very day. She'd been prepared to give the whole sob story of her being lost in the desert for days if the airline had refused to change her flight. That hadn't been necessary. Once she told the woman on the phone her name, the woman had known right away what had happened to her. Apparently, her story had been all over the news. Codie was glad she didn't have any family left alive. They would have been worried sick about her.

Codie found the trip to Toronto, Ontario, Canada, a rough one. Though she'd seemingly had recovered from her ordeal in the desert, she found she grew tired more easily. By the time she reached her apartment all she wanted to do was sleep.

After spending another night without seeing Horus in her dreams, Codie took a long hot shower before rummaging in her kitchen to find something to eat for breakfast. Before leaving on her holiday in Egypt, she'd pretty much cleaned out her fridge, leaving only the things that wouldn't go bad in her absence. That left her choices pretty limited. In the end, she decided to only have tea, which she had to drink plain since she had no milk to put in it.

Once the kettle boiled and the tea sat steeping in the teapot, she went into her small living room and then turned on the television. She pulled open the curtains to the sliding glass doors that lead to her balcony before she sat on the couch.

She flipped through the channels and grimaced as she caught the tail end of a news story about her rescue in Egypt. She continued to change the channel until she found a cooking show. She didn't normally watch television during the day. Talk shows were not her thing, so the cooking show would have to do.

At first, she thought her mind played tricks on her. She heard the cry of a falcon coming from outside her balcony door. Once Codie heard it a second time, she had to look. She crossed the short distance to the balcony door and looked through the glass. She blinked, then rubbed her eyes and blinked again. Perched on the railing of her balcony sat a sooty falcon. As far as she knew, Toronto didn't have any.

Slowly, she unlocked the sliding door and pushed it open. The falcon remained where it perched as it eyed her. Codie slid opened the screen door about to step out onto the balcony when the falcon jumped off the railing and flew past her into her apartment.

Codie swung back around to find the falcon calmly standing in the middle of her living room, staring at her.

She shook her head. "Oh, no you don't. You can't stay here. Out you go." She pushed the screen door open wider, hoping the falcon would take the hint and leave. She didn't want to chase the poor thing out of her apartment.

The falcon didn't as much as move. Codie took a step toward it. She quickly drew up short as the falcon's image shifted and changed. She sucked in a deep breath as her dream Horus took the falcon's place.

She shook her head, not daring to believe he could actually be there in her apartment. Breathing rapidly, she backed away and closed the glass balcony door as she pulled the curtains shut. If she was going to have a break down, she didn't want the whole world to see. Not that anyone would have seen, considering she lived on the sixteenth floor of her apartment building.

Horus smiled and held out his hand. "Come to me, Codie?"

Codie shook her head. Air rasped in and out of her lungs as she breathed rapidly. "You're not real. I know you aren't real. I made you up. All the time spent out in the hot sun must have fried my brain."

"I'm real, Codie. As real as everything that happened out in the desert. Touch me and you'll know I'm not a figment of your imagination."

"Okay."

Codie took a tentative step toward Horus. If she touched him and he disappeared, she'd know she had a screw loose in her head. If she touched him and he was real... She didn't let her mind go down that road just yet.

After taking the last remaining steps that brought her to stand before him, she started to hyperventilate. Codie took a deep breath, trying to slow her breathing. It didn't do any good. Still she hesitated. Horus shook his head at her reluctance, grabbed her hand and placed it on his chest.

At the feel of his heart thumping beneath her hand, Codie really began to lose control. "Oh, god, oh, god. You're real."

Horus pulled her into his arms and pressed her face to his chest. "It's okay, Codie. Breathe."

Codie pressed herself closer. "I thought I would never see you again. I so much wanted you to be real. When I tried calling to you while in the hospital and you didn't come, I thought for sure I made you up."

Horus placed a finger under her chin and tipped her head back. "I heard you call to me, but I wanted to give you the time to recover from your ordeal. I'm sorry if I made you think I didn't hear you. You're my mate. I'll never leave you. I love you."

All the air left her lungs in a *whoosh* at Horus' confession. "Then why didn't you come to me?"

"I wanted you better before you had to make the decision of whether you would want to be my mate or not."

"Of course I want to be—"

Horus placed a finger against her lips before she could finish her sentence. "This is a decision you can't make lightly, Codie. I want you as a true mate. You'd have to give up your life in the mortal realm. Your friends, your family. I'd make you an immortal as I am. I could never let you go once you chose to live with me as my mate."

Codie pulled Horus' finger away. "I want to be your mate, Horus. I love you, more than I've loved anyone else. I have no family. They're all gone. I was raised by my grandmother, and she died years ago. All I have is you."

With a groan, Horus bent his head and claimed Codie's lips in a searing kiss. She clung to him, desperately kissing him back. As their clothes disappeared, she yanked on his thick black hair and practically climbed up his body, needing him inside her. As the floor rose to meet her and he came down on top her, she knew she'd never give up this man, this Egyptian god. At the feel of his hard cock pushing deep inside her, she didn't think an eternity together would be long enough.

The End

JUDGEMENT BY ANUBIS

While in a coma, Jinny finds herself standing before the Egyptian god Anubis to be judged. After shifting from his half-man/half-jackal form, she's instantly attracted to the man, falling for his dark good looks.

Anubis is drawn to the mortal woman he is to judge. As he starts to lose his heart to Jinny, he delays passing judgment, keeping her lingering between two worlds — the realm of the living and the underworld where he dwells.

The longer Anubis puts off his judgment the weaker Jinny becomes until he's forced to make his decision. His choice — he either lets her return to the realm of the living, or allows her to remain in the underworld, which would mean her death.

CHAPTER ONE

Jinny Hunter placed the open sign inside the window of her small bookstore and unlocked the door. She gave the store a final look before she stepped back to stand behind the counter. Today she'd arranged to have a psychic to do free tarot card readings for all the customers who came to her store. She'd sent out flyers to the surrounding neighborhoods, and splurged by putting an ad in the local newspaper in the hopes of drawing a bigger crowd.

It wasn't as if her store did badly. She had a few regular customers, but it by no means earned her the money some of the larger bookstore chains did. Situated on College Street in the city of Toronto, her store was close to both the University of Toronto and Ryerson University, as well as the Royal Ontario Museum. So she usually had a trickle of customers each day.

The bell that hung on the front entrance door jingled. Jinny looked over and smiled at the older woman she'd arranged to come for the day to give the tarot readings. Nepha smiled back as she walked over to where Jinny stood. Jinny came around the counter to greet her.

"You're right on time, Nepha. I'm really looking forward to today. I still wish you'd let me pay you for your time."

Nepha shook her head and said in her Egyptian-accented English, "I don't want your money, Jinny. I'm doing this to help drum up local business. It doesn't make much sense for you to go to all this trouble to bring in customers and then have to pay me the extra profits you'll make from this day. Keep your money."

"I still feel as if I'm taking advantage of you. I'll have to think of way to pay you back some other way." It'd been Nepha's idea for her to do the readings. She'd been coming to the bookstore for the last couple months, at least once a week, and they'd struck up a friendship.

"It's all right, Jinny. I'm doing this because you're my friend. Now where do you want me to set up?"

Jinny pointed to the small table near the counter that she'd moved there the night before. Nepha went over to it and then sat in one of the chairs. She dug around in her large purse before she pulled out her deck of tarot cards. She put the purse down onto the floor at her feet. She took the cards out of their box and then shuffled them in preparation for the first customers to arrive. The older woman handled the cards gently, careful not to bend the corners. Nepha had to be at least sixty in Jinny's estimation. She really didn't know much about her. Nepha had immigrated to Canada from Egypt, and she had a son who still lived in that country. Other than the fact that she claimed to be psychic and could read tarot cards, Jinny didn't know that much else about her.

The bell on the door jingled as the first customer of the day arrived. Jinny left Nepha to greet the young woman. After explaining about the free readings, Jinny left her to roam the store on her own.

Much to Jinny's pleasure the bookstore did a fair amount of business that day with a steady stream of customers. Some of the customers had come just to have their cards read by Nepha, but Jinny didn't mind. At least they'd come to her bookstore, and there could be a chance they'd return to make a purchase another day.

As the last customers of the day left the bookstore, Jinny locked the door behind them. She took the open sign out of the window, which she replaced with a closed one. Nepha still sat at the small table where she'd been all day.

"Well, I have to say the day turned out to be a rousing success, thanks to you," Jinny said to the older woman.

"I have a feeling you'll have some repeat customers."

"I hope so."

Nepha waved her over to the table. "Come sit down, dear. You've been on your feet all day. I'll read your cards."

Jinny sat in the chair across from Nepha. She sighed with pleasure. "It's nice to get off my feet. You don't have to do a reading for me. You did more than your share of readings today."

"I insist. I'll just do a mini-reading for you with one card only. That way it won't take very long. It's getting late, and I know you want to go home." Nepha gathered up the familiar Rider-Waite tarot cards she'd used for the customers. She returned the cards to their box and put it inside her purse. She gave Jinny a smile as she pulled out another deck of tarot cards. "I'm going to use my special cards for you. This is my Egyptian tarot deck that I only use for family and friends."

Nepha pushed the deck in her direction. Jinny picked it up and looked through the tarots. They had a black background with what looked like a piece of papyrus in the center. On the papyrus, the representation of each card had been drawn using an Egyptian theme.

Jinny put the cards back together and passed them back to Nepha. "They're beautiful."

"Thank you. Now let's do your reading." Nepha

shuffled the cards before she split the deck in half and then put the bottom cards on the top. She held her hand over the deck for a few seconds, then pulled the top card and placed it face up on the table.

Jinny looked at the card. On the top right she read the word death. Jinny didn't know much about tarots, but she didn't think getting the death card could be anything but bad.

"The death card," she said with some disappointment.

Nepha tsked. "The death card doesn't necessarily mean literal death. It can mean the end of your old life and the start of a new one."

Jinny pulled the card closer and studied it. On it stood the Egyptian god Anubis in his half human/half jackal form. In one hand he held a jar and in his other a scroll. Behind him stood a very large set of scales. On one scale sat a feather and on the other the figure of a mummified person. If Jinny remembered correctly from the number of times she'd gone through the Egyptian section of the ROM, the museum, Anubis had the job of weighing the hearts of the dead against the feather of truth. If the soul was found guilty, he'd give it to Ammut to consume, and the soul went on to their final death.

"Isn't Anubis associated with death in the physical sense?" Jinny asked.

"Yes, he could best be described as a death god, but for you that isn't the case. The death card marks a new beginning in your life, and Anubis is the key."

"Then I guess having the death card drawn for me means things should start looking up for me. Maybe there'll even be a new man in my life."

Nepha chuckled. "There just may be." She gathered the cards together and then picked up her purse. "I'll leave you to finish closing for the day. I can let myself out. I'll see you next week."

Jinny thanked the older woman, then grabbed one of

the chairs to take to the backroom. After she returned for the second, Nepha had already left. She hefted the table to the back of the store before she went to the counter to collect her purse and keys. As she reached for the ring of keys that sat on top the counter, Jinny found the death card from Nepha's Egyptian tarot deck sitting beside them. She looked in the direction of the door, but Nepha would more than likely already be long gone. She picked the card up and slipped it into the pocket of her jacket. She figured she'd have to wait until she saw Nepha next week to return it. She didn't have a telephone number to contact her. And now that she thought about it, she realized she didn't even know Nepha's last name.

After locking the door behind her, Jinny headed for the small parking lot behind the bookstore. The night air felt cool, smelling as if fall wouldn't be too far off. The early part of September in southern Ontario could be counted on to have a wide range of weather. One day it could be hot as any summer day, then the next rainy and cool. She pulled her lightweight jacket closer around herself against the chill and headed for her car.

She managed to make it almost home to her apartment when a black cat streaked out in front of her car. Jinny didn't see it until she was almost on it. Acting on instinct, she swerved to avoid hitting it, which put her in the opposite oncoming lane of traffic. She only had a split second to register the fact that the bright lights headed her way belonged to another car before it rammed into her head-on. Jinny screamed, then her world went black.

CHAPTER TWO

Jinny blinked as she found herself hovering above a group of what looked like doctors and nurses in a space that had to be a hospital emergency room. They busily worked on whomever lay limp on the bed. Monitors and other machines beeped as one doctor ordered a nurse to prep the patient for a series of tests he wanted done. She hovered closer, wanting to get a better look. What she saw had her shaking her head in denial.

Her body lay bloody and limp on the bed. A tube stuck out of her mouth as one nurse squeezed air into her lungs. IV lines ran out of both her arms, while other lines led to some of the machines that had been attached to her chest. It didn't look good, especially since she'd somehow come to be outside her body. One of the doctors said she'd slipped into a coma. Wanting back inside her body, she tried to get closer, but something pulled her away. All of a sudden her world went dark once more.

After the black receded, Jinny found she was no longer in the hospital room. She stood in the middle of a large shadowed room. Looking down at herself, she saw she still wore the jeans and long-sleeved t-shirt she'd put on that morning. She shook her arms and legs, which felt to be all in one piece. She didn't feel any pain either. She didn't know if she should take that as a good or bad sign.

Unsure of exactly where she was now, she looked around. The walls and floor appeared to be stone. On the walls, what looked to be Egyptian hieroglyphs had been painted or carved into the stone. This couldn't be right. The more she saw the more she couldn't help but think this room resembled an ancient Egyptian temple or a tomb.

A sound drew her attention away from the walls. After spinning in the direction it'd come from, Jinny froze in place. It couldn't be. This couldn't be real. This had to be something her injured brain had conjured while in its coma state. In no way could that be the Egyptian god Anubis who stood a foot away quietly watching. In half-human/half-jackal form he towered over her. His body appeared to be covered in shiny black fur. He wore a snow-white linen kilt around his hips. Dark brown eyes stared back at her.

Anubis reached out to her. "Come." His deep voice seemed to fill the room.

Jinny shook her head. "You're not real, and I'm not dead."

He closed the distance between them and picked up her hand in his. "I'm very real." Anubis cocked his jackal head as he stared at her. "And you're correct. You aren't dead."

She had to crane her neck to look at him now that Anubis stood so close. At five-foot-four, she had to look up at most people, but he had to be at least six-foot-eight.

"Then why am I here if I'm not dead?"

"I'm not sure, but now that you are I still must judge you. You have one foot in the realm of the living and one here in the underworld. It will be my choice either to send you back to the living realm or let you move on."

She drew herself up straighter. "I want to go back to the

realm of the living, thank you very much. I'm only thirty. I still have lots of living to do, and I'm not going to give that up without a fight."

Jinny wondered if she'd gone a little too far when Anubis released her hand and took a step back. Pissing off a god probably wouldn't win her any brownie points, but at the moment, she didn't care. And then there was the question if this place actually existed outside her mind.

Anubis' body wavered and blurred, bringing Jinny out of her thoughts. In seconds, Anubis the man stood in the half-human/half-jackal's place. She slowly took in his long, black hair and muscular build. He still towered over her even in human form. He wore the same snow-white kilt low on his narrow hips. It made her wonder what he had under it. She dragged her gaze up to his face, and her heart pounded. For the god of death, he had a face women would go ga-ga over. Not unaffected herself, her nipples grew taut beneath her shirt as her pussy throbbed. Feeling wetness form between her legs, she knew she was most definitely still alive.

*

Anubis looked at the mortal woman who stared hungrily back at him with her light green eyes. She intrigued him. Most souls who arrived in the underworld were intimated by him, especially seeing him in his half-human/half-jackal form that he used when he judged souls. Not this mortal woman. She not only told him he couldn't be real, she even went so far as to tell him he *had* to send her back to the living realm. He had the feeling she'd fight him if he decided otherwise.

She really was a small thing. She had to be at least a foot shorter than him. She had a slim, athletic build, curved in all the right places from what he could tell. Her looks could only be described as classically beautiful, but she didn't look to be the type of woman who flaunted it. He skimmed his gaze over her long, dark brown hair and then down her body to her feet. Her nipples had pebbled beneath the shirt she wore. He smiled.

"What's your name?"

"Jinny." She continued to stare at him with longing. "And you're the Egyptian god Anubis."

"Yes."

His cock stirred as her gaze quickly flicked down to his kilt for a second time. He smelled her arousal mixing in the air. Much to his surprise, his cock lengthened and thickened. She affected him in ways no mortal had before. He found himself attracted to her. Thoughts of what it'd be like to take her to his bed flashed in his mind. Usually for him sex was something he only occasionally indulged in, and never with a mortal.

"What should I do with you?" he asked.

Her gaze came back up to focus on his face. "Send me back?"

He shook his head. That he couldn't do just yet. He needed time to not only make the right decision, but to get to know this mortal woman who drew him to her. "No. My decision can't be taken lightly. I must have the time to think the matter over. You'll stay here with me for now."

Jinny looked around the sparsely furnished chamber. She gave him a questioning look. "Here? You want me to stay here?"

He chuckled. From her tone of voice, he could tell Jinny didn't relish the idea of having to stay in this chamber. "I don't mean exactly right here. This is the chamber where I judge souls. I have my own private one, which I think you'll like much better."

Jinny blushed. "Sorry. I didn't mean to be rude. It's just kind of dark and gloomy in here."

"Then let me take you to my chamber."

Anubis led Jinny to the back of the chamber and

through a small doorway that connected the judging chamber to his personal one. He took a quick look behind him to make sure she followed and found her staring at his ass. His cock jumped as the tip of her tongue came out to wet her bottom lip.

He stepped aside and allowed Jinny to walk farther into the chamber ahead of him. She stopped in the middle of the chamber and slowly turned in a circle. Her gaze lingered on his large bed before she moved on. Anubis could think of a number of things he'd like to do to her once he got her into that bed. And it wasn't a question of would he get her there, but when.

He knew exactly when she found his bathing pool. With a sound of pleasure, Jinny walked over to it and longingly looked down at it. His thoughts shifted direction. The pool would do just as well as the bed.

CHAPTER THREE

S he felt Anubis watching her as she walked over to the large bathing pool. At the edge, Jinny squatted and dipped her hand into it. It was warm. Large lotus blooms floated on the surface, perfuming the water with their scent. She could just imagine how good it'd feel to strip naked and have a good long soak in the pool.

"By all means, take your clothes off and make use of my bathing pool."

Jinny stood and turned around to find Anubis had come up behind her. "You read my mind?"

"Even if I couldn't, I'd still be able to tell what you were thinking from the look of pleasure you wore on your face."

She swallowed. Anubis stood so close she felt the warmth coming off his body. She licked her suddenly dry lips. The movement drew his gaze to her mouth. Jinny could see the look of hunger that lurked in his dark brown eyes. He wanted her. Her pussy ached, wanting to be filled. She dropped her gaze to his wide, muscular chest, then over his washboard abs. The thought of being able to lick and caress every inch of that bared flesh caused her to breathe heavy. Going even lower, she encountered the very large bulge that tented the front of his kilt. She most definitely wanted to get a better look at what he had under that snow-white material.

Anubis reached out and brushed his hand against her cheek. Once Jinny looked up, he brought it around the back of her neck and pulled her to him. As he lowered his mouth to hers, she angled her head up to meet him halfway. No other man aroused her as much as he did, or so fast. The few boyfriends she'd had in the past had been lukewarm compared to what this Egyptian god made her feel.

At the first brush of Anubis' lips, Jinny sighed and tentatively placed her hand on his chest. His heart pounded beneath her palm. Needing to be closer, she took a step in until the tips of her breasts touched his skin. She brushed them back and forth, which sent shockwaves of pleasure to her pussy. With a growl, he snaked his other arm around her waist and yanked her tighter against him. His lips slanted against hers as he pushed his way inside her mouth.

She felt every hard inch of Anubis as he held her firmly to him. The hard ridge of his cock lay nestled against her stomach. Jinny reached between them and cupped his erection. It jumped as she squeezed him.

Anubis lifted his head and pulled away. "How about we continue this in the bathing pool?" He took her hand and led her to the one end of the pool that had steps leading into it.

Jinny kicked off her shoes. She reached for the hem of her shirt. Anubis placed a hand on hers before she could lift it. He shook his head and moved her hands aside.

"Let me do it."

She nodded and took her bottom lip between her teeth as he slowly pulled her shirt up her body, over her head and dropped it to the floor. He reached out with a finger and swirled the tip around each of her nipples through the lace cups of her bra. Jinny bit back a moan as Anubis took a taut nipple between his fingers and rolled it with a slight tug.

Once he removed his hand and seemed to hesitate as if he didn't how to remove her bra, Jinny reached around her back and unhooked it. She pulled the straps over her shoulders and let it slip off her arms to join her shirt on the ground. Anubis smiled as he cupped one of her bare breasts in his large hand. He bent his head and flicked her nipple with his tongue. She couldn't hold back the moan that slipped past her lips. She arched her back and pressed closer in invitation, wanting to feel his warm mouth against her skin. He made a sound of encouragement as he laved her nipple before he sucked it deep inside his mouth.

Jinny nearly went up onto her toes as he sucked at her breast. With each hard pull of his mouth, she felt it deep inside her pussy. The wetness between her legs increased, dampening the material of her panties. Anubis shifted to her other breast, giving it the same attention. She tunneled her fingers through his long, black hair.

Inching lower, Anubis dragged his tongue along her ribs, then nibbled a trail down to her bellybutton. There, he swirled his tongue inside it. Going down onto his knees before her, he undid the button and zipper of her jeans. He took hold of the waistband and slowly inched them down her hips. He tugged over her legs and off, taking her socks with them. Now only in her panties, Jinny gazed down at him. He stared back up at her as he brushed her clit with the backs of his knuckles. She felt her own wetness as he rubbed them back and forth against her panties.

Anubis pulled his gaze away and hooked the top of her panties with his fingers as he pulled them down her legs. Jinny kicked them away. He ran his hands along the tops of her thighs, then back up the inside, slightly spreading her legs. A finger ran along her pussy.

"I want to see if you taste as sweet as you smell." His

voice sounded rough with need. He bent his head and laved her clit as he held her legs open. "Hmm, you do taste sweet." He buried his face between her legs.

Jinny moaned as she clutched Anubis' wide shoulders. Her legs shook as he licked her pussy. She rocked her hips against his mouth, and he flicked her clit with the tip of his tongue before he sucked on it. Her orgasm raced up to meet her. She was so close to coming. As if he sensed it, he moved away and stood. She whimpered.

Anubis reached for his kilt. With swift motions, he pulled it free of his body. He removed the loincloth he wore under it. Jinny's inner walls clenched as he stood there gloriously naked. He was all muscle. His large cock jutted out from his body, fully engorged. As she watched, he took hold of himself and ran his hand up and down his length a couple times before he grabbed her hand and then led her into the water.

The warm water rose higher as she walked down the stairs beside Anubis. At the bottom, it came to sit just beneath her breasts. After he went to the center of the pool and ducked under the water, Jinny sunk into it as well. She broke the surface to find him gliding toward her. He'd slicked back his wet hair, allowing her to see more of his rugged, handsome face.

He reached for her and pulled her closer so he could hold her against him. Jinny shifted until she had the hot, hard length of him between her legs. She leaned up to take Anubis' mouth in a heated kiss, rubbing herself along the length of his shaft. She moaned as she thought of how good it'd feel to have it buried inside her, stretching her, filling her.

Already completely aroused, Jinny clutched his shoulders as she wrapped her legs around his waist. She whimpered with need and angled her hips, trying to get the tip of his cock to the opening of her body. Anubis grabbed her bottom and stilled her movements. He continued to kiss her while he walked over to the stairs. After reaching the second step from the top, he turned and sat. The water lapped at his sides as he positioned her knees on the step on either side of his hips.

No longer able to wait, Jinny broke their kiss to rise on her knees as Anubis took hold of his cock and led it to the entrance of her body. With her bottom lip between her teeth, she slowly impaled herself on his thick shaft. They both moaned as he filled her to the hilt. She lifted and then pulled back until he was almost free of her body before she sank on him once again. She tortured them both a few more times with slow, lazy strokes. She clamped her inner walls around him and picked up the pace. Her breasts jiggled as she rode him harder. All too soon her climax overtook her. Moaning loudly, she came, her inner muscles clutching his hard length.

After the last spasm receded, Anubis rose with Jinny in his arms, their bodies still joined. He walked over to his bed. She wrapped her legs around his waist as he followed her down onto it. Once he settled his weight above her, he moved inside her. Even though she'd already come, another orgasm built as he plunged into her. His pace grew faster, and his cock grew harder inside her. The head of his shaft hit her cervix with each stroke in. Shifting higher up on her, he angled his hips so his thickness rubbed her clit as he pumped in and out of her. She pushed her head down onto the mattress and lifted her hips to match his pace. He stiffened above her and groaned. His cock pulsed deep inside her as he came. She quickly followed, crying out as an intense orgasm swept through her.

Anubis collapsed on top of her. Jinny wrapped her arms around him and held him tight. He soon rolled to his side and tucked her head under his chin as his now flaccid manhood slipped free of her body. Resting her head against his shoulder, Jinny let her eyes flutter shut. A wave of contentment washed over her as she snuggled closer. Satiated and completely relaxed, she drifted off to sleep.

CHAPTER FOUR

Anubis looked down at the small mortal woman he held in his arms. Never before had he felt such pleasure, such a connection to another. Whenever he'd indulged in sex in the past he'd enjoyed it, but it, by no means, compared to making love to Jinny. Hearing her cry out as her body shattered around his only increased his desire. His own release had been so intense it'd seemed to go on and on. He brushed a lock of her damp hair away from her face and then kissed her forehead. She didn't stir. The longer he watched her sleep, something swelled deep inside his chest that made his breath catch.

Even though he'd never experienced the feeling before, he knew what it meant. Jinny was his mate. The other half to his soul. Anubis pulled her closer as what she truly meant to him filled his heart.

He'd longed for a mate for thousands of years. Having to judge souls, and dealing with death on a daily basis, he ached to have someone to take away the darkness that part of his life created. Could he keep Jinny with him?

She sat in limbo. A part of her remained in the realm of the living while she dwelled there in the underworld with him. He didn't really know how long she could remain. Most souls only stayed long enough to be judged before meeting their true death or moving on to the next realm. What he did know for sure was he didn't want to let her go. And when he made his final judgment about Jinny that would be exactly what he'd have to do. If he decided she had to pass on to the next realm, to him she'd be dead. If he let her return to the realm of the living, she'd be alive, but he couldn't go there to be with her. He also had the option of making her immortal and then taking her as his mate, but she'd have to live there with him. Could she live with death always around her? He didn't think she could. And he couldn't leave the underworld. It was forbidden.

Anubis closed his eyes and breathed in Jinny's scent. He found himself in a quandary. He didn't know if he could let her go. Not wanting to think about it any longer, he held her to him as she slept, relishing the feel of her in his arms.

* * * *

Jinny stretched as she slowly came to wakefulness. The last thing she remembered before falling asleep was the feel of Anubis' strong arms holding her close. She smiled as she thought of their lovemaking. He'd put all the other men she'd slept with to shame.

She turned her head to look at the spot next to her, and realized she slept alone in the large bed. Anubis' pillow still held the indent from where his head had lain, but as she reached out, she found the sheets on his side of the bed cool to the touch. He must have gotten up some time ago. Being an immortal and an Egyptian god, it made her wonder if he actually needed to sleep.

Jinny sat up and stretched again. She glanced over at the bathing pool. She felt her face flush as she thought of what she and Anubis had done in it. She wouldn't mind having a second round.

Not sure where Anubis had gone or when he'd return, Jinny decided to take another dip in the bathing pool. She slipped off the bed and walked over to the stairs. She sighed as the warm water lapped at her skin. What she wouldn't give to have one of those in her apartment. After sinking under the perfumed water, she swam the short distance to the other side. She broke the surface near where one of the lotus blooms floated. Its flowery scent filled her lungs as she bent to smell it.

Jinny leisurely swam back over to the stairs and then climbed out of the pool. She looked around the chamber and found a large stack of fluffy towels piled on a table against one of the walls. She took one off the top and then toweled her hair and body dry. Once she no longer dripped water all over the floor, she wrapped the towel around herself. It was then she heard voices coming from the judging chamber. Curious, she quietly walked over to the entrance way that joined the two chambers and peeked around the corner. She made sure to keep most of herself hidden behind the wall.

Anubis stood in the middle of the chamber in his half-human/half-jackal form. A set of large scales that hadn't been in there when she'd arrived stood next to him. She noticed the small lineup of people standing before him. The first person, an older man, came forward and passed him what looked to her to be a heart. Jinny silently mouthed the word eew as Anubis took the heart and placed it onto one of the scales. On the other already sat a feather. The scales swung from one side to the other until it hung exactly in the middle, perfectly balanced. The man smiled with pleasure as Anubis motioned him to move to a spot to his right. The older man disappeared.

The next person in line also was a man, but much younger in years. As the older man had done, he too gave Anubis his heart, which in turn he placed onto the scales.

This time when they slowly stopped moving the heart weighed heavier than the feather. With a growl, Anubis took the heart off the scale and went to something that slunk in the dark shadows near the back wall. Jinny shivered as goose bumps rose all along her skin as whatever the thing was made a snarling noise as it took the heart from Anubis. She heard sloppy, munching sounds. Shuddering in disgust, she quickly looked over at the man being judged. He let out a piercing scream and vanished.

Unable to look away, Jinny stayed to watch Anubis judge the two remaining souls. Luckily for them, when their hearts were weighed, they stayed balanced on the scales against the feather. After they left the chamber, she looked up to find him watching her. He remained in his half-human/half-jackal form as he crossed the distance between them. She stared at him as he came to stand in front of her.

Jinny took in the large ears that sat atop his head and his pointed muzzle. She found he appealed to her in this form almost as much as he did in his human one. Crazy, she knew, but there it was. As she gazed into his eyes, she saw the real Anubis staring back at her. Maybe that was why she wasn't disgusted by that form. Something in his eyes drew her closer.

She wrapped her arms around his waist and rested her head against the soft black fur on his chest. "It bothers you to have to do that. To have to sentence a soul like that, even if they deserve it."

Anubis wrapped his arms around her waist. "Yes. I don't enjoy having to feed the heart of a wicked soul to Ammut to be devoured. You really don't mind being around me when I'm in this form, do you?" His voice held a touch of incredulousness.

Jinny lifted her head and leaned back only far enough so she could look at him. "Of course not. This form is a part of what you are. You make it sound as if no one has touched you when you've been like this."

"That's because no one ever has. Most of the other gods won't even look at me when I take on this form."

"Well, that's their loss. You're all soft and furry." Jinny ran her hands up his chest to his collarbones. "I could pet you like this all day."

Anubis closed his eyes and growled low in his throat. "It'd be no hardship for me."

Jinny could tell he enjoyed her touching him. Growing bolder, she moved her hands higher and gently caressed the top of his muzzle. He bent his head to give her better access when she stroked still higher to caress each of his ears. She pressed her lips to the side of his muzzle and dragged her hands down to the side of his neck and then to the tops of his broad shoulders. Following the same path as her hands, she pressed kisses along Anubis' collarbones to the slabs of muscle padding his chest.

As she went down his chest, Anubis shifted back to his human form. Sleek fur gave way to smooth skin. Jinny circled his flat nipples with her tongue as his kilt and the towel she wore disappeared. Pressed skin-to-skin, the hard length of Anubis' cock snuggled against her stomach. She inched her way lower, taking the time to explore every inch of him with her lips and tongue. On her knees, she reached around him and dragged her nails down his muscled ass as she kissed a path across his rippled abs. He moaned and cupped the back of her head, urging her to go lower still.

With a smile against his skin, Jinny complied. Leaving his abs, she focused her attention on his thick erection. She took hold of his cock and squeezed it as she ran her hand up and down the shaft. He grew harder with each pump of her hand. She kept it up until a small bead of moisture appeared on the very tip. She stilled her movement, but keeping her grip on him. She leaned forward and licked the drop off with the tip of her tongue. Anubis groaned and pushed closer. He mumbled something she thought had to be in Egyptian, because she didn't understand any of it. From the way he spoke, she figured they had to be words of encouragement.

Not that she needed any. Desire coursed through her as wetness trickled down the insides of her thighs. Knowing her touch caused Anubis to shudder with desire only amplified her own. That she, a mere mortal, could have such an effect over a god made her want him even more.

With a firm grip on the base of his shaft, Jinny licked his cock from base to head. At the tip, she circled it. Anubis' hips jerked in response. She opened her mouth and took as much of him as she could handle inside. As she squeezed him, she slid her mouth up and down his shaft, sucking hard. He dug his fingers into her hair at the back of her head as he rocked into her mouth. She moaned against his skin.

Anubis suddenly reared back and reached for her. He picked her up into his arms and took her mouth in a demanding kiss. He walked with her until he had her pinned against the wall. As his tongue tangled with hers, he reached between them, positioned himself and entered her in one hard stroke. Jinny locked her ankles around his waist and held on as he thrust into her. The stone wall dug into her back, but she didn't care. All that mattered was the pressure that built inside her with each pump of his hips between her legs.

He rode her, he cupped her bottom with one hand and reached between them with his other to rub her clit. "Come for me, Jinny. I need to feel your body clutching mine as you come. You feel so good."

He surged into her hard and continued to work her clit. Jinny squeezed her inner muscles around his thick cock as he filled her over and over again. With a keening moan, she climaxed. Anubis slammed into her one final time and held her to him. There was a splash of hot liquid once his cock pulsed deep inside her.

After Anubis let her stand on her feet, Jinny found her legs shook. She didn't know if she'd be able to walk. He scooped her up into his arms and then took her to the bed. Once her head hit the pillow, she suddenly felt utterly exhausted. She didn't think she could move, even if her life depended upon it. It felt as if someone had dropped a heavy sheet of metal on top her, pinning her where she lay. Tiredness sucked at her, pulling her ever deeper. She vaguely noticed him slipping into the bed beside her so he lay on his side next to her. On her back, she wanted to roll over to her side and snuggle against him, but it seemed like too much work for her. Giving up the fight, she fell into a deep, dreamless sleep.

CHAPTER FIVE

There really was no night and day in the underworld. Anubis usually only slept the few hours his body required when he felt tired. With Jinny asleep at his side, he let himself relax. He ended up sleeping for almost two hours. After he awoke, he found her still asleep. Mortals needed a lot more sleep than immortals, and he figured with part of her still in the realm of the living, she'd need to rest longer than he had. Even though he didn't need any more, he didn't get out of bed. He wanted to stay close to her.

He didn't want to give her up, especially now. What he'd told her about no one ever touching him in his half-human/half-jackal form had been the truth. That one was too closely associated with death. The other immortals in particular didn't want to deal with any aspect of mortal demise. That Jinny didn't mind that part of him, and actually could bring herself to touch and kiss him in that form, filled a lonely, dark place in his heart. He wanted forever with her, but he couldn't expect her to live in the underworld. She wouldn't be able to thrive there with the souls of the dead who came to be judged.

Looking down at Jinny, he caressed her cheek with the tip of his finger. Her skin felt a little cool to the touch. His brows drew together in concern. Anubis pulled her to him. She didn't stir. He put his hand over her heart. It beat in a steady rhythm, skipped a beat, then went back to a steady beat again.

After putting Jinny back down flat on the bed, Anubis shook her. "Jinny, wake up." When she didn't respond, he shook her harder. "Jinny, you have to wake up now."

She finally took a deep breath. Color appeared on her cheeks as she blinked her eyes up at him. "I'm so tired, Anubis. Can't you let me sleep a little bit longer?"

Jinny's eyes drifted shut again, but he didn't allow her to go back to sleep. "No, you can't sleep anymore. You have to stay awake."

She must have picked up on the urgency in his voice because her eyes snapped open. "What's wrong? Why do I have the feeling my being so tired is a bad thing?"

Anubis sat up and pulled her onto his lap so her head rested against his chest as he held her tight. "Souls aren't supposed to remain in the underworld, Jinny. This is just a stopover point, the way station if you like, before they move on to the next realm or meets final death. The longer you stay, the weaker you're going to become. Already it's having an effect on you. That's why you're so tired, and why your skin felt cool to the touch."

Jinny reached up and caressed his cheek. "What would happen if I stayed?"

He shook his head. "I really don't know. You're the first soul that has stayed for any length of time. I have a feeling it'll weaken you until you'll no longer exist in any realm."

"That isn't good." She slipped off his lap to kneel beside him. She cupped his face in her hands. "I don't want to leave you, Anubis. I know this is going to sound cornball, but I think I love you. I think from the first time you touched me. Can't we be together in some way?"

Anubis sadly shook his head. "No, we can't. If I let you go on to the next realm, you'll be dead to me."

"What about if you send me back to the realm of the living? Can't you come to me there?"

"It's forbidden, Jinny. I can't leave the underworld. It's my task to judge all the souls who come to the underworld. Mine alone."

"So you're going to give me up." She said it as a statement rather than a question.

"I don't want to. I love you as well. We're meant to be together. You're my mate. I've waited centuries for you, but I'd rather give you up than let you become a lost soul."

Tears welled in Jinny's eyes as she came to terms with what he must do. Leaning toward her, Anubis kissed her like a starved man before he got out of the bed. He needed to be alone while he decided what his final judgment would be for her. He gave her one last look of longing, willed his kilt back onto his body, then left her alone.

* * * *

Jinny roughly brushed away a lone tear that slipped down her cheek. She punched the mattress. It was all so unfair. She finally found a man she wanted to spend a lifetime with, and she couldn't keep him. She didn't want to leave the underworld, but she had to agree with Anubis. She was already growing weaker the longer she stayed, and she'd only grow more so.

Tears threatened to rise as she thought of not ever seeing Anubis again once she left there. Even though they'd really only been together for a short period of time, she felt a connection to him. He'd become a part of her. Once she left the underworld, it'd be as if she'd left a piece of her behind. It'd hurt like hell. One thing Jinny knew for sure—she'd never forget him. Ever. And she doubted there would ever be another man in her life. How could she love an ordinary man when she'd already given her heart to an Egyptian god? She couldn't.

Time ticked by, and Anubis didn't return. He'd left to be by himself, to decide what would be her fate. That would take a toll on both of them. As she waited, she started to feel lethargic. It'd be all too easy to let it sweep her away, but she fought its pull. She went into the bathing pool, hoping the water would help keep her awake. She did lengths under the surface. It helped a little, but she still felt it on the very edge of her consciousness, waiting to claim her.

Jinny climbed out of the pool and then vigorously dried her hair and body. Looking around, she tried to see what had happened to her clothes. She spotted them neatly folded at the end of the bed. They hadn't been there before she'd gone into the pool. She pulled them on and looked up to find Anubis standing in the doorway in his half-human/half-jackal form, watching her. The time of her judgment had arrived.

* * * *

Jinny followed Anubis out into the judging chamber. As always, it was cloaked in shadows. She pointedly ignored the dark corner where Ammut had been when Anubis had earlier judged the other souls. Once they reached the middle of the room, he turned to face her a short distance away. She swallowed hard. She fisted her hands at her sides, her fingernails biting into her palms. She'd get through this without crying. His last memory of her deserved to be of her looking at him with all the love she felt for him in her eyes, not her blubbering like an idiot.

"No scales?" Jinny asked him softly. "I thought you needed them when you judged souls."

Anubis shook his head. "I don't need them this time. The scales are for souls who need to be judged before they can be let into the realm after death."

"You're sending me back?"

"I can't say that out loud yet. If I do, you'll leave."

Unable to stay away any longer, Jinny crossed the small distance between them and threw herself into Anubis' arms. "I don't know if my heart can take it. It's already starting to hurt, and I haven't even left yet." She rubbed her cheek against the black fur on his chest.

He wrapped his arms around her and rested his jackal head on top hers. "You'll be okay, Jinny. Just remember, I'll never forget you. You'll always be my mate."

Gently, Anubis pushed her away. Jinny's eyes blurred with unshed tears. "I'll always love you, Anubis."

Their gazes collided, then Anubis said the words to send her back to the realm of the living. "I now give my final judgment of this soul. It isn't her time. I return her to the realm of the living."

Jinny called out Anubis' name as she was suddenly pulled out of the judging chamber.

CHAPTER SIX

Jinny came awake and started to choke on the tube that had been put down her throat to help her breathe. Panicking, she groped for it. In her weakened condition, she only managed to dislodge one of the lines that were stuck to her chest. A machine beeped loudly as an alarm went off.

A couple of nurses came running into her hospital room a few seconds later. One of them rushed over to her as the other went to shut of the alarm. Jinny continued to choke as she fought to breathe against the tube.

The nurse pulled her hands away. "Relax, dear. You have to breathe with the machine until we can get the tube removed."

Unable to get past the sensation of choking, Jinny's heart raced. The nurse who hovered over her yelled for the other to get a doctor. He arrived in no time at all with a syringe in his hand. He quickly stuck the needle into one of her IV lines and then pushed the plunger home. Jinny instantly grew still as whatever the doctor had given her took effect. A second later, her eyes closed and her world went black.

* * * *

The next time Jinny awakened the tube had been removed from her throat, allowing her to breathe on her own. She spent the next two weeks in the hospital, recovering from her injuries. She'd been lucky, or so the nurses had told her. All she'd really sustained from the accident was a really good bump on the head that had put her in a coma. Her car had been a total write-off.

While recuperating, she had a lot of time to think about Anubis. She wanted to be with him so much. At times it hurt worse than the leftover headache from her head wound. She'd never see him again. She knew that. It'd just take her a while, if ever, to come to terms with it.

Once she finally could leave the hospital, Jinny went home to her lonely apartment. She had no family. She'd grown up in an orphanage. All she knew about her biological parents was that they'd been teenagers at her birth, and had chosen to give her up. They also had made it quite clear when they'd signed the legal papers to have her put into the orphanage that they wanted no contact with her once she came of age. Having basically lived alone for most of her life, she'd never forced the issue.

As per her doctor's orders, she waited a couple days before she opened her bookstore again. It'd sat closed the whole time she'd been in the hospital since she couldn't afford to hire someone to work with her. The loss of business while she'd been laid up would hurt, but she hoped to make up for the lost time.

Jinny arrived at her bookstore bright and early. Fall had arrived while she'd been in the hospital, bringing a definite chill to the air even during the day. After stepping inside the store, she didn't feel much difference between the inside temperature from that of outside. Once she flipped on the lights, she headed to the back to the thermostat. She cranked on the heat and then rubbed her arms against the chill. She decided to leave her jacket on until the place warmed up. She headed over to the counter to store her purse beneath it. Once behind it, something that sat on top the counter caught her attention.

With her eyes focused on the object, she put her purse away. Her hand shook slightly as she picked up the Egyptian tarot card. It was the same death card Nepha had left behind the night of her car accident. Jinny wondered how it came to be back there. She distinctly remembered putting it in her jacket pocket before she'd left the store that evening. The card had been lost. One of the nurses at the hospital had taken her jacket in to be dry cleaned to remove the blood from her accident. After she'd returned it, Jinny couldn't find the tarot card in her pocket.

Jinny lovingly traced the figure of Anubis on the tarot card with her finger. She blinked back the tears that threatened to rise to the surface. The artist had done an excellent job of capturing him in his half-human/half-jackal form. Taking a deep, she put the card back down. She'd have to give it back to Nepha when she eventually came to the bookstore, but Jinny found herself reluctant to do it. She wanted to keep it for herself.

A steady trickle of customers came to the bookstore throughout the day, which made Jinny feel a bit better about her finances. Every little bit helped. An hour before closing time, the bell jingled above the front door, announcing the arrival of a customer. She looked up from the stack of invoices she'd been going through. Nepha hurried over to her, came around the counter and pulled Jinny into her arms for a hug.

"I've been so worried about you, Jinny dear. Are you okay?"

Jinny gave Nepha another hug before she stepped out of her embrace. "I'm okay now. I guess it'd been a bit touch and go in the beginning. How did you know about my accident?"

"I read about it in the newspaper right after it happened. I would have come to visit you in the hospital, but I thought it best to let you recuperate in peace."

"It's the thought that counts, Nepha." Reluctantly, Jinny picked up the Egyptian tarot card off the counter and then held it out to the older woman. "You left this behind the day you did the tarot card readings."

Nepha shook her head and pushed it back toward Jinny. "You keep it."

"I can't do that. If I keep it, it'll break up your deck."

"I insist. Don't worry about it. I can always get another deck. I think the card means more to you than it does to me. Am I right?"

Jinny nodded, not trusting her voice at first. "Yes. It has come to mean a great deal to me."

Nepha looked at her closely. "You've met a man. One you've come to love."

"Yes, I have. We just can't be together. I guess it wasn't meant to be."

"Nonsense. If he felt just as strongly about you, the both of you should try to work something out."

"It's a bit more complicated than that."

Nepha patted her cheek and smiled. "Don't mourn, Jinny. Your mate will come for you."

After that cryptic remark, Nepha left the bookstore, leaving Jinny to wonder how she could have known that only one person had ever called her his mate — Anubis.

* * * *

Anubis couldn't stop thinking about Jinny. He missed her, more than he thought he would. He longed to be with his mate. It sometimes overshadowed everything else in his life. She'd already been gone a few weeks, and he didn't know how he'd last an eternity without her by his side. He'd also come to realize how lonely his life had been before she'd come into it. Now, it'd become repetitive and dark. He no longer wanted to judge the souls who arrived in the underworld. Being around death day after day took its toll on him. He'd had a taste of the light in the form of Jinny, and he wanted it back.

With a sigh of longing, Anubis pushed thoughts of Jinny aside as he faced the latest batch of souls to arrive. He reached for the heart of the first and then placed it on the scale. When the scales balanced, he sent the soul on to the next realm. As the last man stepped forward and offered him his heart, Anubis barely gave him a glance. After the scale dipped, showing the heart weighed more than the feather, he felt no emotion at all as he gave it to Ammut to consume. Nor did he react when the soul screamed in terror just before he disappeared.

Anubis shifted back to human form and headed for his personal chamber. He quickly shed his kilt and then climbed into the bathing pool. He needed to wash away the taint of death. It was a figment of his imagination, the souls didn't carry the scent of death on them when they came to be judged, but that didn't stop his skin from crawling.

Like every other time he'd gone into the pool, Anubis remembered what he and Jinny had done in and around it. He stood in the middle and closed his eyes as he became aroused. Inside his mind he heard the cries Jinny made as she came beneath him. His cock jerked under the water as he remembered how it'd felt when she'd taken him inside her mouth, how it'd felt to sink into her warm body as she cried out her pleasure. He resisted the urge to reach down and give himself some relief. It wouldn't be the same. He opened his eyes and cursed as he slapped the surface of the water.

He ducked under and swam to the stairs. Once Anubis broke the surface, he saw he was no longer alone. His father, Osiris, stood at the bathing pool's edge, watching him. Not caring that his father would easily be able to see how aroused he'd become, Anubis climbed out of the water, walked by him and picked up a towel to dry himself with.

"Shall I come back at a better time?" Osiris asked with a smile as he eyed the state of Anubis' body.

Anubis wrapped the towel around his waist. "No, Father. Why have you come?"

"Do I need a reason to visit my son?" At Anubis' raised brow, Osiris shook his head. "I'll admit I don't come to see you enough. I decided to do so now because I've felt your unhappiness."

"There's nothing you can do, Father."

"I beg to differ. I know you had to give up your mate. I've come to make you a proposition."

That Osiris knew about Jinny didn't surprise Anubis. His father knew most of what happened in the underworld. "And what would that be?"

"I'm willing to take your place in the underworld. As the caretaker and protector of the dead. That way, you may go to your mortal mate and live with her in the realm of the living, permanently."

Anubis's heart raced at the possibility of being able to live with Jinny. "Why would you do this for me?"

Osiris shook his head. "Must there be a reason? I'm only thinking of my child's happiness. Your childhood wasn't the best."

His childhood had been strained at its best. His birth mother had tricked Osiris into her bed, where she became pregnant with him. After giving birth, his mother had given him to Osiris and his wife, Isis, to be raised as their own.

"If I accept, when would you release me of my duties?" he asked.

"As of right now. You'd be free to leave to go to your

mate whenever you wanted to. And before you can ask, you'll retain your godhood and immortality, even though you'll live among mortals. You'll lose none of your powers."

With a nod, Anubis whipped off the towel he wore and willed a kilt onto his body. "Then I accept."

Osiris smiled. "I wish you much happiness with your mate, my son."

Anubis bent his head in his father's direction, then flashed himself to the realm of the living.

CHAPTER SEVEN

Most of another week went by. Jinny slipped into her old routine of life. She got up in the morning, opened the bookstore for business, stayed until night, then returned to her apartment to watch a few hours of television before going to bed. She'd wake up the next morning to start all over again. Her life hadn't seemed boring to her until now. A big chunk of herself seemed to be missing, and no matter what she thought to do to compensate for it, it remained as an empty hole in her soul.

Jinny stood by the bookstore's front window and eyed the new display of books she'd been arranging. She tried to change the display once every couple weeks, in the hopes to lure customers into the store if a particular book caught their eye. Happy with it, she looked out the large window. Evening had started to descend. She watched the heavy traffic go by as people rushed to go home after a long day at work. She envied those who had husbands or wives at home, waiting for them to return. All that waited at her place for her was her television set.

Business had been kind of on the slow side that day.

Even though she had no big plans for the rest of her night, Jinny decided to close the bookstore early. With a sigh, she went to the back of the store, turned off the lights, then turned on the dim security lights that she left on after closing. As she turned back around, Jinny's breath caught in her throat. There in the middle of the bookstore stood what at first glance she thought had to be a dog, but after a second look, she knew it couldn't be one. The animal's legs were too lanky. It had large pointed ears on top its head, and its elongated jaw made her think it had to be a jackal, an Egyptian jackal to be exact. She'd done enough research on the Internet about them since her return from the underworld she knew she had to be right in her thinking. The only difference between this jackal and the ones she'd researched was the color of the fur. Most Egyptian jackals had fur ranging from gray-beige to dirty yellow. This jackal had fur black as midnight.

"Anubis?" Jinny whispered, not daring to hope it could actually be him.

The jackal slightly bent his head. Jinny sucked in a breath, then quickly went and put the closed sign out in the window. She turned back from locking the door to see the jackal watched her intently. It had to be Anubis. The dark brown eyes that looked back at her were the same.

"Let's go to the backroom," Jinny said. "Even with the lights off too many people can see inside the bookstore."

The jackal followed on her heels as she walked to the backroom, flipped on the light and closed the door that connected the back from the front of the bookstore. Her heart pounded as the jackal's form wavered and blurred. Her chest rapidly rose and fell as Anubis the man took the jackal's place.

"Are you really here? I thought you couldn't leave the underworld."

Anubis' gaze hungrily raked her body before he looked into her eyes. Jinny gasped at the intense longing that lurked in their depths.

"I'm really here, Jinny. And I'm here to stay, to claim you as my mate. If you'll still have me. My father, Osiris, relieved me of my duties so I no longer have to remain in the underworld. I can stay in the mortal realm with you forever. Will you have me as your mate?" Anubis opened his arms wide.

With a cry of joy, she threw herself into them. "Of course I'll have you as my mate. I just can't believe you're actually here."

Anubis cupped her face in his hands and made her look up at him. "Then I'll accept nothing less than an eternity with you."

Out of the corner of her eyes, Jinny noticed Anubis' hands glowed. A surge of power jolted through her where he touched. It zipped through her, seeming to fill every cell in her body. She looked at Anubis. "Did you just make me like you? I don't feel any different on the inside, but I definitely felt you do something to me."

Anubis smiled and brushed his lips against hers. "You're immortal now, Jinny. I won't have anything separate us now, not even death."

A shudder of longing racked Jinny at Anubis' words. Her blood heated as wetness pooled between her legs. She'd no longer be alone. She'd have forever with the man she loved. Leaning forward, she kissed him with everything she had to show him how much she'd missed him.

With a growl, Anubis moved his hands down to her waist and hauled her up against him. Their tongues dueled as Jinny reached up to thread her fingers through his long, black hair. His erection nestled against her stomach. She ached to have the hard length of his cock buried inside her pussy. It didn't matter that they were in the backroom of her bookstore. All that did was getting him inside her, riding her hard as she called out his name.

Anubis lifted his head and smiled at the stark desire that had to be showing in her eyes. "I need to be inside you, Jinny. I'm going to pleasure you until all you can think of is having my cock buried deep inside you. You won't know where you end and I begin. First, I want to taste you as you come against my mouth."

Jinny's breath caught as the erotic imagines that Anubis described filled her mind. He backed her up until her bottom hit the edge of the office desk. He roughly shoved what sat on top it to the opposite side, perilously close to the edge. She only had time to be thankful her computer was on a small table next to the desk before he reached for the buttons of her blouse and then opened them one by one. He yanked it off, then undid her jeans. They too quickly ended up in a pile on the floor at her feet. Her bra and panties followed suit.

Anubis' gaze raked her from head to toe. He reached for her and then lifted her to sit on the edge of the desk. She tried to take hold of the kilt he wore, to pull it off him, but he stepped back. He shook his head and shifted between her spread thighs. He cupped her breasts and lifted them as he dragged the flat of his tongue across each of her taut nipples. Jinny arched her back and whimpered.

Anubis continued to tease her. He licked her nipples, swirling his tongue around each tight bud, refusing to take them into his mouth. When she couldn't take anymore, she tunneled her fingers through his hair as she rubbed a nipple against his lips in offering. He growled deep in his throat as he opened his mouth and sucked it deep inside. Jinny moaned and ground her pussy against the large bulge in his kilt.

As he continued to suck at her breast, Anubis took a step back. He ran a finger along her pussy. He groaned as he pushed two fingers inside her core, coating them with her wetness. Jinny whimpered as he thrust them in and out of her. She rocked her hips in time with his thrusts as her orgasm inched ever closer.

Jinny cried out as Anubis' fingers suddenly left her body. Her nipple popped out of his mouth as he went down onto his knees in front of the desk. He pulled her closer to the edge and then put her legs over his broad shoulders. She cried out again as his mouth took the place of his fingers. He lapped at her pussy as he spread her legs even farther apart. The sight of his dark head between her thighs had her moaning. It wouldn't take much to send her over the edge. Unable to sit up on her own any longer, she leaned back on her hands. He stiffened his tongue and jabbed it into her core over and over again. She rocked her hips against his mouth. Once he took her clit between his lips and sucked, she let out a keening whimper when she climaxed.

After the last spasm took her, Anubis rose between her spread legs. His kilt disappeared. Jinny moaned at the sight of his large cock standing out from his body. A bead of moisture sat on the head. She licked her lips. He groaned in response. Aching to be filled, but wanting to touch him first, she sat up and rubbed the bead of pre-cum into his skin. She wrapped her hand around his thick shaft and slowly worked it up and down his length. He moaned and he wrapped his hand around hers, squeezing to let her know he wanted her to increase the pressure of her grip.

Jinny inched closer until the head of his cock entered her body. Still working her hand up and down his shaft, she rocked her hips, riding the very tip of him. She squeezed her inner muscles around it and moaned. Anubis' control snapped. He pulled her hand away, positioned himself and thrust his shaft deep inside her. Leaning over her, he forced her down onto her back as he took her bottom in his hands and pistoned between her thighs. She wrapped her legs around his waist. She quickly came again as he surged into her. He increased the pace as his cock grew even harder. Once he reached his climax, he threw back his head and roared, holding her to him, spilling deep inside her.

It took a minute for Jinny to catch her breath. Once she could speak, she said, "Let's go home, Anubis."

He lifted off her and pulled free of her body. He gave her a look that said he liked the sound of that. "Home. Yes, let's go home."

His kilt was suddenly back around his hips, and she once again wore her clothes. Jinny eyed him. "It may take a bit of explaining to the taxi driver why you're walking around barely dressed in the fall."

Anubis chuckled. "We don't need a taxi, Jinny. I'm still a god. Egyptian gods don't take taxis."

"They don't?"

"No, we don't."

"Then how are we getting home?"

"If there is anything you need from here, I suggest you get it."

With purse in hand, Jinny learned firsthand what Anubis had meant. In a blink of an eye he had them inside her apartment. Two seconds later, he swept her into his arms and took her to bed. He proceeded to keep her too busy to ask any more questions.

CHAPTER EIGHT

Two days later, Jinny couldn't be any happier than she already was. Since Anubis had arrived on a Saturday evening, and she never opened her bookstore on Sundays, they'd spent most of that day in bed making love. They'd only come up for air long enough for her to get something to eat. Even though now immortal like him, she wasn't a goddess, which meant she still needed to eat and sleep as she'd done as a mortal. He'd explained that to her after her stomach had growled loudly after a bout of lovemaking.

That night as they sat on the couch, watching television, naked, Jinny mentioned the fact that Anubis would need mortal clothing if he had a chance of fitting in. He quickly assured her it'd be no problem since he could will his clothes onto his body, in any style. To prove it, he willed on a pair of tight-fitting jeans and a snug long-sleeved t-shirt that showed off his powerful body. She'd proceeded to strip them off, which lead to more lovemaking on the couch.

Now Monday, both she and Anubis were at her bookstore. He'd decided he wanted to work there with her. Sitting home alone all day while she went to work held no appeal to him, he'd said. Jinny figured it was a perfect arrangement, especially given the fact she could watch him all day. As she did right now. She leaned back against the counter as he put books on a shelf. The muscles in his arms bunched with his movements.

He turned and looked at her. "If you don't stop looking at me like that, I'll have to take you to the backroom and put your desk to good use again."

Jinny gave him a heated look. "I'm going to close for lunch in a half hour. We can make use of it then."

Anubis chuckled and turned back to finish putting books on the shelf. He continued to work as the bell jingled above the door. Jinny smiled as Nepha walked over to her.

"I see you're much happier, Jinny. I told you everything would work out in the end. I knew your mate would come for you."

Nepha turned and looked at Anubis, who stared at the older woman. He put the books he held down and came over to stand before her. "Mother?"

Jinny looked from Anubis to Nepha. She stared in shock as Nepha's image wavered. One minute Nepha was the familiar older Egyptian woman she recognized as her friend, and the next a much taller and younger woman was in her place. Nepha the younger was also breathtakingly beautiful.

"Hello, my son."

"What are you doing here?"

"I found Jinny for you. I knew she'd be perfect as your mate. And the more I came to know her, the more I became convinced she'd be the one."

Jinny couldn't stop staring. "Nepha?

"My true name is Nephthys. I'm the Egyptian goddess of mourning."

"You made it so I had that car accident, didn't you?"

Nephthys nodded. "It couldn't think of another way to have you and Anubis meet. I'm sorry."

"Why did you do all this, Mother?" Anubis asked, drawing the goddess' attention back to him.

She smiled. "You deserved to be happy. I felt your restlessness. I may have given you up to Osiris and Isis, but I've never stopped watching over you, Anubis. Now you've found your mate, and you're free to live here in the realm of living with her. Be happy, my son."

Nephthys took a step back as if she meant to leave. Jinny quickly hugged the goddess. "Thank you, Nephthys, for giving me Anubis."

She hugged Jinny back, then stepped away. "I'm proud to call you my daughter, Jinny."

Jinny smiled as Anubis wrapped an arm around her shoulders and pulled her up against his side. "If you're leaving now, Nephthys, you have to make me one promise before you go."

"What would that be?"

"That you'll continue to see us at least once a week. I'll miss you if you don't."

Nephthys smiled and nodded. "Then I'll see you next week."

Once the goddess disappeared, Anubis turned Jinny in his arms and held her close. She snuggled against his chest. Her life couldn't have turned out any better. She'd found her very own Egyptian god, and thanks to a certain death card, she'd have forever with him.

The End

SEF, LION OF YESTERDAY

Separated from his twin when a demon traps them in the mortal realm, Sef falls for the mortal woman who nursed him back to health while trapped in his lion form. Unable to return to the underworld where he and his brother, Duau, guard its gates, Sef fears an attack that is sure to come.

A vet, Chandra takes in many exotic animals that have been mistreated by owners who don't know how to look after them. After she accepts the lion that had been captured in a farmer's field, she sees something in his eyes that reaches out to her. Never did she expect the lion to shift into Sef, one half of the Egyptian god Aker.

When the demon finds Sef and takes him and Chandra to the underworld, she has to make the ultimate sacrifice for the man she loves.

CHAPTER ONE

Sef called out to his twin brother, Duau, as he placed himself between the gate to the underworld and the large group of demons who faced him. Duau appeared at his side a split second later.

As twins, he and Duau were virtually identical. Both of them had dark brown hair, that they both wore shoulder length, and gold eyes. They stood at six-foot-ten. Along with their height, their bodies had a thick padding of muscle, which they needed since they each guarded a gate where the sun god Ra entered and exited the underworld each night.

The demons' eyes glowed red as they slowly inched closer. Sef growled in warning. "We won't allow your kind to pass through the gate."

The demon who stood out in front, who Sef assumed was their leader, returned his volley. "I didn't ask your permission, guardian. We're prepared to go through you if need be to get through the gate."

At their leader's signal, the demons drew their swords as one. In answer to the threat, Sef and Duau quickly shifted into their lion forms. They didn't need swords to defend the gate. In the form of Barbary lions, they each weighed six hundred pounds of pure muscle. Their weapons of choice—razor-sharp teeth and claws.

They roared as the demons suddenly went on the attack. Sef bunched his powerful back legs under him and launched himself at the closest one. He brought the demon down before he even had time to raise his sword. Sef tore his throat out with his powerful jaws just as another demon came up behind him. He roared in pain as he took a sword cut across his one shoulder. He turned to face his attacker and then swatted the demon with one of his massive paws. The demon went down hard, which gave Sef the chance to move in for the kill.

The battle raged on. He and Duau roared as they fought the demons. They took them down one at a time until only the leader remained alive. Sef and Duau circled around him as they hemmed him in on both sides. Blood from the wounds they'd received marked their fur in places.

The leader's eyes burned red. They stalked closer. "You may have defeated the others, but I get the last strike," the demon said.

The demon raised his hands in their direction. Sef roared with rage as he realized the demon had called upon some power to pin him in place. Duau roared as well as he fought the demon's hold. The demon laughed at their futile attempts to break free. He recited a spell. Sef fought even harder. The demon sought to separate him from Duau, and trap them both in the mortal realm. Just as the demon completed the spell, Sef only had enough time to look at his twin before they were yanked from the underworld.

* * * *

Chandra Marshall finished inspecting the large thoroughbred gelding and then patted his neck. He really was a beautiful horse, not that he'd looked it when he'd first arrived. Malnourished, as well as mistreated, the gelding had been in bad shape. What a difference the right amount of food and some loving care had made.

After closing the stall door, Chandra went to her next patient. A veterinarian, she ran her own animal rescue shelter, something she'd always wanted to do. Once she'd graduated, she'd worked for a couple years in a veterinarian clinic, only long enough to save up money to buy a place large enough to start her shelter. At twenty-eight, she now lived her dream on a medium-sized farm on the outskirts of Toronto.

The sound of a phone ringing caused Chandra to change direction. She quickly headed to the back of the large barn where she had a small office.

On the fourth ring she picked up the phone. "Animal Rescue Shelter."

"Hey, Chandra, it's Bill."

"Hi, Bill. What can I do for you?"

"Do you have room to take on another animal?"

"Sure do. What do you have for me this time?" An animal lover, Bill had found many injured or mistreated animals over the years, which he brought to her to look after.

"I have a lion for you this time."

"A lion?" She'd taken care of a few wild cats since she'd opened the shelter, mostly lynx, bobcat and cougar, but never a lion.

"Yes. A male lion to be exact. We have him tranquilized, but he's in rough shape. He has some pretty deep wounds. He needs your magic touch."

"Where did you find him?"

"I'll explain more when I get to your place. I'm on my way as we speak. I should be there in about five minutes. I knew you wouldn't turn him away. See you in a bit."

Chandra hung up the phone after Bill clicked off. She

headed back out to the main part of the barn to check the large kennel she'd used to house the other cats. It'd be a bit on the small size for a full-grown male lion, but it'd hold him. The sound of Bill's van coming up her gravel drive had Chandra rushing outside to meet him.

Bill climbed out of his white cargo van and then waved as she approached. Once she joined him, he took her around to the back of the van and opened the doors. Chandra's breath caught at the sight of the large male lion stretched out asleep on the van's floor. Bill's wife, Violet, sat with the lion's head in her lap. Both in their early sixties, they looked more like grandparents, which they were, than tough and canny animal rescuers.

Violet smiled. "Good to see you again, Chandra. Our boy here has had a pretty rough time of it from the looks of him."

Chandra looked the lion over as she made note of the dried blood on his coat. The wounds looked to be slice marks, as if someone had taken a large knife to him. "Let's get him inside the barn. I'll open the back doors, Bill, if you want to drive around."

As Bill climbed back inside the van, Chandra hurried to open the large sliding doors at the back of the barn. She'd have Bill back right up to the kennel. Hopefully the three of them would be able to get the lion out of the van and into it. He'd would weigh a ton. Male lions could be several hundred pounds.

Somehow the three of them—along with the aid of the rolling table she used when she did surgery—managed to get the large lion out of the van. Luckily, he didn't come out of the tranquilized-induced sleep while they moved him. They'd had to manhandle him a bit more than Chandra would have liked, but there had been no going around it. After assuring Bill and Violet she'd have the lion fixed up in no time, and that she'd keep them informed of his progress, she waved them off.

She returned to the barn and then grabbed the things she'd need to clean up the lion's wounds. Chandra headed back to the kennel. She'd have to work quickly. He could come out of it at any time. In no way did she want to be inside the small space with a fully aware full-grown male lion. It may not be the safest thing to do, to work on the lion alone, but she didn't have an assistant to help her. The animals she had in the shelter usually weren't the dangerous type. And she preferred to work on her own.

As Violet had said, some of the wounds turned out to be on the deep side. She couldn't shake the feeling that someone had taken a really large knife, or sword, to him. A couple looked as if they could be stitched, but for now she settled on only cleaning the wounds. She'd wait and see what they looked like tomorrow. Giving him more tranquilizers when she didn't know how much Bill had already used on him wouldn't be a good thing. If she gave him too much, there would be a chance he'd never wake up.

Chandra had almost finished when the lion twitched as she cleaned one of his deeper wounds. She debated whether to leave the last wound or to quickly take care of it. Once he seemed to relax again, she decided to just quickly get it over with. That turned out to be a mistake. As soon as she touched the wound he went from being under to completely awake and standing on all four paws. He moved his head right up into her face and gave her a good sniff. She stiffened. She was so screwed.

CHAPTER TWO

Chandra sat very, very still. Right now the lion didn't look as if he'd go on the attack, but she didn't want to take the risk of setting him off. He took a small step back, then after a few seconds, he roared and shook his head as if in denial. She tried very slowly to inch closer to the entrance to the kennel on her bum. If she could make it outside, she could get the gate shut and lock him inside. He swiftly went to stand over her and looked at her with his gold eyes as she leaned back on her hands.

"Nice, lion," she said softly. He cocked his head to the side at the sound of her voice. "You don't want to bite me. I'm only trying to help you. Some nice people brought you to me to look after your wounds. You don't want to bite your doctor."

As if he understood what she'd said, he turned his head to look back at himself. She swore he checked out a particularly deep wound that ran along his side. After a quick look, he swung his head in her direction. Her heart beat faster as her fear threatened to overtake her. With a deep breath, Chandra pushed it aside. If she showed her fear, the lion would possibly attack her.

He suddenly lifted a paw, which happened to be bigger than her hand, and gently tapped her cheek with it. Chandra bit back a whimper. In response, he shook his large head and put his paw back down. Much to her surprise, he butted his head against her chest much like a house cat would do when it wanted to be petted. Once he did it a second time, she lifted a shaky hand and scratched him behind his ear. A noise that sounded more like a growl/purr filled the kennel each time the lion exhaled. It seemed to grow louder the longer she scratched him.

"You like that, don't you?"

She smiled as he came closer. She lifted her hand and scratched his other ear as well. He leaned against her and purred with contentment. Chandra continued to scratch behind his ears for a few minutes longer. For such a large cat, this lion acted as if he were nothing more than an overgrown house cat. Feeling it'd be safe now to move, she dropped her hands and then gathered up the supplies she'd brought into the kennel to treat him. He watched her as she walked to the end before she took hold of the door to shut him inside. A large paw shot out and pushed it back open once she started to close it.

Chandra shook her head. "Sorry, but I can't have you wandering around loose."

He looked up at her, and their gazes met. As the lion held hers, she suddenly found herself unable to lock him in the kennel. She somehow knew he wouldn't do anything to hurt her, and that he'd be more comfortable if she took him to the house with her instead. She shook her head, but the need to keep him close didn't go away, as if the idea had taken root and wouldn't be denied.

Stepping back, Chandra moved aside so he could walk out of the kennel. He seemed steady enough when he stood, but once he walked, she could tell the tranquilizer still affected him. She let him lean against her leg as she first got rid of the supplies in her hands and then headed out of the barn.

She opened the front door of her house, a two-story brick farmhouse, and let the lion go in ahead of her. Darkness had started to fall as she'd looked after his wounds. Chandra could already hear the crickets through the open windows. After going into the kitchen, she looked at the clock on the stove. Almost six. She turned to find the lion at her feet as he patiently watched her.

"Are you hungry? I know I am. How about I fix us both something to eat?"

Of course he didn't answer her. Chandra didn't have any raw meat to give him. What she had was frozen in her freezer, but she did have a few cans of dog food kicking around. It wouldn't be the lion's normal fare, but it'd have to do. She crossed to the pantry cupboard and then took out one of the cans. After she opened it, she put it all into one of her mixing bowls before she filled another with water. She set the bowls down in front of him and waited to see what he did with them. The lion completely ignored both of them and continued to stare up at her. She shrugged. She'd tried.

With the lion now taken care of food wise, she decided to get something for herself. After a quick look in her freezer, she settled for a frozen TV dinner. Once she had it heating in the microwave, Chandra sat at the kitchen table to wait. The lion continued to watch her every move. She studied him in return now that she didn't fear he'd pounce on her.

Her brows drew together as she took in the lion's mane. It appeared to cover more of his body than an African lion's. It ran down his chest, through his front legs and down his back to below his shoulders. The mane around his face was blond, while the rest was a very dark brown, almost black. Chandra had been able to spend a day with one of the vets who worked at the Toronto Zoo a few years back. On that day, one of the male lions had needed one of his front paws operated on. She'd been able to get up close and personal to him once they'd brought him in and he'd been tranquilized. There were definite subtle differences between the lion she'd seen in the zoo and the one now in her kitchen.

The microwave beeped, and Chandra went to get her dinner. She left it on the counter to cool a bit before heading to the living room to get her laptop. She placed it on the kitchen table and then booted it up. While she ate, she went on the Internet. She typed in the description of the lion's mane into a search engine. What came up surprised her.

As Chandra had started to suspect, this lion wasn't an African lion. According to the information she pulled up, he had to be a Barbary lion, which had her shaking her head. The Barbary lion's natural habitat had been in North Africa, from Morocco to Egypt. They were extinct in the wild now with only a few true Barbary lions found in zoos. How the hell had a full-blooded Barbary lion come to be loose on a farm in rural Ontario? From the picture on the Internet taken of a Barbary male lion, the one that currently watched her matched the picture.

After she finished her meager meal, Chandra poured herself a glass of wine and then headed to the living room to watch some television before she went to bed. She woke up shortly after dawn to take care of the animals she had out in the barn, so bedtime came early for her.

She sat on the couch and switched on the television. The lion hopped up beside her and then stretched out with his head on her lap. Chandra just about jumped out of her skin when he shoved his nose between her legs and sniffed.

She pushed him away. "Stop that." He did it again, but this time he dragged his raspy tongue along the crotch of her pants. She pushed him away once more and shook a finger at him. "There will definitely be none of that going on, mister. I don't even let guys I go out with on first dates get that close. Not that I've had many first dates lately, but still, behave yourself."

He turned and licked her fingers before he lay back down with his head on her lap. This time he kept his head facing in the direction of the television. Chandra absently stroked his head as she skipped through the channels until she found something of interest to watch.

Once she found herself nodding off a few hours later, Chandra decided she'd better head up for bed. She nudged the lion until he lifted his head off her lap and sat up beside her.

"Well, big boy, time for bed. I know you're comfortable on my couch, but I'd prefer not to have you wandering around the house while I sleep. You're going to sleep in the laundry room tonight."

Chandra got up and then went to the front hall closet to collect one of the old blankets she stored there. With the lion at her heels, she went back to the kitchen and opened the door to the main floor laundry room that sat off the kitchen. She spread the blanket on the floor and then looked down at the lion. He'd followed her inside.

"Make yourself at home, and I'll see you in the morning." After closing the door behind her, Chandra went upstairs to bed.

CHAPTER THREE

Sef watched the door close behind the mortal woman. He wished she hadn't closed him inside the smaller room, but he did understand why she didn't feel comfortable allowing him to roam around the house while she slept. She didn't know he was more than just an ordinary lion. And right now, he couldn't shift to his human form. Already weakened from the battle with the demons, thrown into the mortal realm and then hit with something that had put him to sleep, he couldn't make the change. He still felt a bit on the groggy side. Once whatever the other mortals had given him completely left his system, he felt sure he'd be able to shift. He hoped.

He lay down on the blanket and wondered what had happened to his twin. After he'd arrived in the mortal realm, he'd found Duau no longer with him. He'd tried to call out to his brother, but he'd gotten no response. Either the spell the demon had used to send them to the mortal realm prevented it, or something had happened to Duau and he couldn't answer. Sef hoped it wasn't the latter.

With his paws, he bunched up the blanket as he shifted

into a more comfortable position. He thought of the woman asleep upstairs in her bed. He wished he could join her and do all the things to her body that swirled inside his mind. Stuck in his lion form, Sef's sense of smell was much better than when in his human one. One whiff of the woman's scent, and the lion part of him had roared with longing. The lion recognized her as his mate. When he'd managed to smell her woman's scent between her legs, it'd just reinforced that she belonged to him.

If he'd been able to shift, he would have taken her to bed and claimed her as his own. The lion wanted to roar with frustration. Sef reined that part of him back. Right now, he needed sleep to regain his strength, and hopefully his ability to shift. Picturing what it'd feel like to have the woman naked under him as he buried his cock to the hilt into her welcoming wet heat wouldn't do him any favors.

He finally slept, but not for very long. As with all Egyptian gods, he only required a couple hours of sleep to recharge his body. Sef stood on his hind legs as he leaned against one of the white machines in the room. Looking out the one window, he saw day had yet to come. He jumped down and then paced the small room. As he did, he tried to contact his brother. Same as before, he received no response back from Duau. Sef couldn't help but worry something had happened to his twin.

Sef continued to pace. Now that he'd slept, he felt stronger, but he held off trying to shift for a couple reasons. First, he didn't want to become frustrated if he tried too soon, and the second, he wanted to shift to his human form in front of his mate. To show her what he truly was.

Another hour went by, and Sef couldn't stand to be locked up in this smaller room any longer. Unlike a true lion that wouldn't have any idea how to work the doorknob, he had that knowledge. He sat up on his hind legs and placed a paw on either side of the knob. He applied pressure and slowly turned it to the right. The door opened into the other room as he used his body weight to push it wide.

Sef padded out of the kitchen and then headed for the stairs to the upper level. He followed the smell of his mate's scent up the stairs and to the very end of the hall. Her bedroom door stood wide open. Silently, he entered the room and went around the bed until he stood at the side where his mate lay sleeping on her side. He skimmed his gaze over her long, blonde hair that lay spread over her pillow. In sleep, her lush lips were slightly parted. He couldn't see her blue eyes, but he could easily see the fan of her dark blonde lashes against her cheeks. He found her beautiful. With a purr, he licked her cheek.

*

Chandra came instantly awake at the sound of a loud purr, and the sensation of a raspy tongue being dragged across her cheek. She sat bolt upright and reached for the lamp that sat on the nightstand next to the bed. As light flooded the room, she met the gold-eyed gaze of the lion who should still have been closed inside her laundry room.

"How did you get out? Now where am I going to put you until morning?"

She sat up straighter as the lion's body blurred. Transfixed, Chandra watched as a man soon stood in the lion's place. Her jaw dropped open, and he stared back at her with marked desire showing in his gold eyes. She slowly took in his shoulder-length dark brown hair, which happened to be the same length as her own, and his tanned muscular body. He wore a snow-white kilt low on his hips and nothing else. By the way she had to crane her neck to look up at him, she knew he had to be tall, even taller than her six feet.

"You can put me in your bed until morning." He spoke in a deep accented voice that seemed to go right through her in a good way.

"What?" With all that delicious male body bared to her view, Chandra found it hard to concentrate.

He smiled, making his male model good looks even more spectacular. "You asked where you were going to put me until morning. How about in your bed?"

"My bed? Who...what are you?"

"My name is Sef. I'm one half of the Egyptian god Aker."

Her nipples pebbled beneath her pajama t-shirt, and Sef gazed at her breasts. "A god? You're an Egyptian god?" She had to admit he looked the part, standing there in nothing but his linen kilt.

"Yes. My identical twin brother, Duau, and I are known as Aker. We guard the gates to the underworld."

Holy shit, there are two of them?

"And because you're a god, you can shapeshift into a lion?"

"Yes. You ask a lot of questions."

"I tend to do that when I'm nervous." Chandra's mouth went suddenly dry as Sef reached for his kilt and yanked off both it and the loincloth he wore under it. Unable to stop herself, she looked down his body and swallowed. His cock stood full and erect from his body. She squeaked as he lifted the covers and then slipped in beside her. She quickly moved over to the other side. "What are you doing?"

Sef shifted to lie on his side, propped up on his elbow. "You're my mate." He reached out with one muscular arm and wrapped it around her waist as he pulled her down next to him. He tucked her against his large body.

Chandra gasped at the feel of his hard cock pressed against her thigh. She responded to his nearness. A rush of wetness pooled between her legs. It'd been so long since a man had held her in his arms like that. And never one as good looking as Sef.

"I'm your mate?" She bit back a moan when he stroked down her waist and then across her ribs to settle his hand just below her breast.

"Another question," he said with a chuckle. He leaned in and buried his face into the crook of her neck as he took a deep breath. "Your scent tells me that you are. I want to be inside you, taking you as mine. I want to hear you cry out as I pleasure you."

A shiver of desire made Chandra shake at Sef's words. Oh, she wanted him as well. Right now, her body didn't care what he was. It just wanted him to put that hard cock of his deep inside her pussy. Pump it in and out of her until she came again and again. She told her body to behave, but it wanted none of that. It'd been too long denied to say no to what he offered. That she found him devastatingly attractive didn't help, either.

Sef made the same purring sound as he'd done while in lion form and nuzzled the side of her neck. His licked her skin as he kissed a trail up to her mouth. Chandra's eyes drifted shut at the first light brush of his lips against hers. Once he took her mouth fully, she gave up the fight. The man knew how to kiss. His lips took hers in a fiery kiss as he pushed his inside. He tasted like pure sin. As his tongue dueled with hers, she wrapped her arms around his neck and pulled until he came to lay half on top her body. Never one to hold back after she made a decision, she jumped in with both feet. She'd deal with the consequences, if any, in the morning.

After threading her fingers through Sef's long hair, she held his mouth to hers as she eagerly kissed him back. He moaned, and she sucked his bottom lip between her teeth and gently bit it. She arched her hips against his erection.

Sef lifted his head and looked at her with eyes dark with passion. "I want to take things slow."

Chandra took his hand and shoved it inside her shirt, placing it on her breast. "More kissing and less talking. I can think of quite a few other things you can do with your mouth right now besides using it to talk."

She reached between their bodies and wrapped her hand around Sef's thick shaft. Squeezing, she pumped it up and down his full length. As if a damn broke, he growled deep in his throat and pulled her shirt over her head and off. Her pajama bottoms quickly followed. Pressed skin-to-skin, he shifted down her body as he kissed a trail to her breasts. He sucked a taut nipple deep inside his warm mouth and settled between her legs. With one hand, he cupped her bottom and lifted her. The head of his cock brushed against her slick opening. Chandra moaned. She tried to lower herself onto his erection, but he held her away to lave her other breast before he sucked it deep.

Chandra dug her nails into his shoulders while Sef continued to tease her. He ignored her and continued to kiss his way down her body. By the time he reached her hips, she panted with need. His wide upper body spread her legs farther apart as he moved lower on the mattress. He purred and nuzzled the inside her thigh. At the first swipe of his tongue along her aching pussy, she just about came off the bed. With her hands fisted in the sheets, she arched against his mouth. He cupped her bottom and lifted her to him.

The sound of her moans filled the bedroom. He flicked her clit with the tip of his tongue. Her core fluttered, and her orgasm inched closer. It'd been so long since a man had made her come that it wouldn't take much to send her over the edge. She whimpered as one finger pushed between her slick folds. When a second joined it, moving in and out while Sef sucked on her clit, Chandra practically screamed as she came against his mouth.

Once the last wave of pleasure diminished, she pulled

Sef's hair until he moved higher on her body. She kissed him, tasting herself on his lips. With a push, she rolled him onto his back. Straddling him, she rubbed her wet pussy up and down the length of his hard cock to coat him with her juices.

She smiled. "My turn to make you come."

She dragged her nails down his smooth chest and across his flat nipples. Sef groaned and arched beneath her. Chandra did it again, but this time when he arched up into her, she angled her hips so the head of his cock butted against her core. Pressing down, she slowly took him in inch by inch. Once she'd taken all of him, she sat up and rode him. His thick shaft filled her, making her moan.

Sef took hold of her hips and surged up to meet each of her downward strokes. Her clit rubbed against his pubic bone, causing her body to tighten as another orgasm built. Chandra clutched his shaft with her inner muscles and increased her pace. His cock grew even harder, and he groaned. All too soon, her orgasm rushed up to meet her. On a long moan, she shattered around him. Her inner walls squeezed his cock in a tight fist. He thrust up into her one last time, almost lifting her off the bed, as he came and filled her with his cum.

Chandra collapsed onto him. Completely sated, she shifted until she lay curled up along Sef's side with her head pillowed on his chest. He held her close, and she drifted off to sleep.

CHAPTER FOUR

O nce he could breathe normally again, Sef looked at the woman he held in his arms. She was his mate in every way. He liked that she took what she wanted, and hadn't been afraid to use his body to find her own pleasure. It'd heightened his own, giving him an intense release that he'd never experienced before. Even now he craved to take her again, but she needed her rest. Dawn soon would be there.

He ran his fingers through her long, blonde hair. It felt like silk, as did her soft skin. Sef suddenly realized he didn't even know her name. In his hurry to claim her as his mate, he'd neglected to ask her. He'd have to remedy that when she woke up, before he made love to her again.

As his mate slept, Sef tried to once again contact Duau. Still his twin remained silent. His brows drew together with worry. He didn't know what he'd do if something had happened to his brother that might keep Duau separated from him. Since their birth, they'd never really been apart. Even though Duau guarded the exit gate to the underworld, as he guarded the entrance, they'd always been able to communicate with each other. They truly were two halves of a whole. Along with his worry for Duau, Sef couldn't stop thinking how the gates to the underworld no longer had guards to stand watch. He needed to return to take up his duties, as well as try to find Duau.

He also had to figure out how his mate would fit into his life. As a mortal, she couldn't survive living in the underworld. Unlike some of the other gods, neither he nor Duau had the ability to give a mortal immortality. They only had the power to remove the causes of death from the dead who came to the gates, asking to be let into the underworld. She'd have to remain in the mortal realm, and he still had his duty. Something would have to be arranged so they could be together, but Sef pushed that thought aside. He'd worry about that when the time came. Even though they'd made love, she still hadn't told him she'd accept him as her mate. That would be something else he'd have to ask her.

A loud beeping sound suddenly filled the room. His mate stirred and groaned. She lifted herself onto her elbow and squinted at the small table that sat next to his side of the bed. With a grumble, she practically climbed over him until she lay sprawled across his chest and then pushed something on the object with glowing numbers. The beeping stopped. With another grumble under her breath, she moved as if to get out of bed.

Sef pulled her back on top him and gave her a sexy smile. "Where are you going? I thought we'd make love again. I still hunger for you." To show her, he pressed his lengthening cock against her.

"Forget it, buster. I'm not going to let you tempt me to stay in bed. I have work to do. Work first, then fun and games after it's finished."

Sef let her slip out of bed. Naked, she headed for the bedroom door. "Are you sure I can't get you to stay?" He yanked back the covers and gave her a good view of his fully engorged cock once she turned around.

"Now you're just not playing fair, but my answer still has to be no. I'm going to take a shower now before I become too tempted and change my mind, which won't get the animals out in the barn fed."

As she turned to leave the room, Sef stopped her. "Can you at least tell me your name?"

She looked over her shoulder and cringed. "Sorry about that. I guess you distracted me last night. I'm Chandra. Chandra Marshall. I won't be long in the shower and then you can have it."

Sef flipped back the covers over him as he watched Chandra's shapely ass disappear out into the hall.

* * * *

After her shower, Chandra dressed in jeans and a t-shirt. She showed Sef the bathroom, and how to work the shower, before she headed downstairs to make a pot of tea. As she waited for it to steep, she thought about the Egyptian god upstairs in her shower. If she hadn't seen him shift out of his lion form with her own eyes, she wouldn't have believed it. What she really wanted to know, though, was how he'd ended up in his lion form in that farmer's field. And why hadn't he shifted to his human one when he'd been spotted.

Never one to eat breakfast, Chandra poured herself a large cup of tea and then sat at the kitchen table while she sipped it. A little while later, Sef came down and joined her.

She eyed the kilt he wore and shook her head. "I hate to say this, considering how good you look in that kilt, but you're going to need something else to wear."

Sef looked down at himself and then back up at Chandra. "My kilt isn't appropriate for the mortal realm?"

Chandra shook her head. "Not even close. Beside the

fact it's the middle of September, and the mornings are a bit on the cool side here in Ontario, you kind of stand out in the kilt. It'll warm up by this afternoon, but it's a tad on the chilly side right now."

"Then what do you suggest I wear?"

"Jeans and a t-shirt would be good, but I don't have any men's clothes kicking around." Chandra blinked as Sef's kilt disappeared to be replaced by tight-fitting black jeans. A tight gray t-shirt now covered his upper body.

"Is this better? I saw a man inside the box we watched last night wearing clothes such as these."

"It's perfect." If anything, the jeans and t-shirt made Sef look even sexier. She still couldn't believe she'd actually slept with him. "Are you hungry? I can quickly fix you something before I go out to the barn."

Sef pulled out the chair across from her and sat. "I don't require food."

"Ah. I guess you being an Egyptian god and all you wouldn't need to eat."

"That's correct."

Chandra took a sip of tea. "Sef, how did you come to be here in the mortal realm? And why did you stay in your lion form until last night?"

Sef picked up one of her hands and held it in his as he rubbed his thumb across the inside of her wrist. "My brother, Duau, and I guard the gates to the underworld. I guard the entrance where Ra enters it at the end of each day. That's why I'm called Sef, which means yesterday in Egyptian. Duau guards the exit. His name means tomorrow. It's also our job to let the souls of the dead through the gates. Since we can open them, a group of demons attacked us. Duau and I fought them in our lion forms. We defeated them all, except for their leader. He used a spell to send us to the mortal realm. Already wounded from my battle, the spell weakened me even more so I couldn't shift."

That explained the wounds he'd had as a lion, which she knew for a fact Sef no longer had. She guess being an immortal he healed a lot faster than a mortal did. "Being hit with a tranquilizer, the drug that made you sleep, probably didn't help, either."

"No, it didn't. Once it left my system, I could shift again."

"What happened to your brother? Bill and Violet, the couple who brought you to me, didn't mention there being a second lion."

Sef shook his head. "I don't know. We became separated. Usually we can talk to each other telepathically, but Duau hasn't answered any of my calls. I need to find him."

"What will you do if you can't?"

"I'll have to return to the underworld without him. The gates have to be guarded against demon kind. I can't afford to stay indefinitely in the mortal realm. I must return."

Chandra drained the rest of her tea and then went to rinse her cup in the sink before she put it into the dishwasher. Hearing Sef say he had to return to the underworld made her realize she'd miss him when he left. She gave herself a mental kick and told herself to smarten up. They'd only slept together once, and it wasn't as if he'd pledge his undying love to her or anything. Even though he'd called her his mate it still didn't mean he wanted to form a long-standing relationship with her. Let's face it, an Egyptian god and a mortal didn't stand a chance of lasting for any real length of time. For now, she'd just settle for the great sex they had together.

Sef came up behind her and pulled her back so she leaned against his chest. "I sense my mate doesn't like the idea of my leaving."

Chandra turned in Sef's arms to face him. "How can I be your mate? We come from two very, and I mean very, different worlds."

"You are my mate. You make me feel things I've never felt before. You complete me in every way. The first time I smelled your scent I knew you were mine."

"You barely know me. I'll admit we hit it off in bed, but the rest, I don't know. I could drive you nuts after a while. My personality sometimes gets on peoples' nerves. I tend to say how I feel, and take what I want. I've lost more than one boyfriend because of it."

"I like that you'll take whatever you want, especially when it's me you're taking." Sef cupped her bottom and pulled her against the large bulge in his pants.

Chandra stepped out of his embrace. "Down, boy. Behave. I told you the animals have to be taken care of first. After that we can have our fun."

"Then I suggest you hurry up. I may not need to eat, but there is a part of you I hunger to taste."

With her body on fire, Chandra grabbed Sef by the hand and quickly led him out to the barn.

CHAPTER FIVE

Sef trailed behind Chandra as she looked in on each of her patients. She had a couple sheep, a goat and a horse in stalls inside the barn. She thoroughly checked the sheep and goat before she dumped some food into the trough set up in their stalls. The horse had his head stuck out over the open half of his as he watched her work.

As they drew closer, the horse suddenly whinnied and reared back as his eyes rolled in fear. Chandra quickly grabbed the horse's halter and then ran her hand down his neck as she tried to calm him down.

"Whoa, boy. What's gotten into you?" She turned to look over at Sef. "He's normally not so high-strung."

Sef stepped away from the stall. The horse quickly grew calm once again. "I think I'm the problem. He must be able to smell the lion's scent, and it's setting him on edge."

"You're probably right. Horses tend to spook easily that way. I'll quickly finish with him and then I have to go up to the loft and throw down some bales of hay for when I feed them again later today."

"You enjoy what you do, taking care of animals?" Sef

asked as Chandra stroked the horse's neck.

"Yeah, I do. I wanted to be a vet from a very young age. I was forever bringing home injured birds. I drove my mom nuts," Chandra said with a laugh.

Sef fell into step beside Chandra after she picked up the now empty feed bucket and then headed to the other side of the barn. "Do you have other family besides your mother?"

"Yes. I have a younger brother as well as my father. I see them when I get a chance, but not as often as my mother would like. They live a couple hours away. What about you? Do you have any other brothers or sisters other than Duau?"

"No. Duau is the only family I have."

"Sorry to hear you lost your parents. That must be rough."

Sef shrugged. "I never knew them, so it doesn't bother me. It's enough that I have Duau."

He stepped back as Chandra climbed up the stairs that led to the hayloft above. She took hold of one of the bales and carried it to the edge. She dropped it to the barn floor below. While she'd been busy looking after her animal patients, the sun had risen higher, causing the air outside to warm. Sef climbed the stairs to the loft as she continued to throw down the bales. At the top, he waited until she turned to head back down to the barn floor before he made his move.

Snaking an arm around her waist, Sef hauled Chandra up against him so they stood touching. "Now that you're finished with the animals I get to have the fun you promised."

Chandra opened her mouth to say something, but he quickly cut her off with his lips. He pushed his tongue inside and thoroughly tasted her. With a low growl of need, he rocked his erection into her. She moaned, threaded her fingers through the sides of his hair and kissed him back. Their tongues twined, tasting each other. Sef walked her backward away from the hayloft's edge and into the middle of the stacked bales. Before he laid her down onto the hay, he conjured a soft blanket big enough for the both of them.

Stretched out on it on their sides, Sef lifted Chandra's leg and hooked it over his hip and ground his throbbing cock against her pussy. The lion inside him roared, wanting to take his mate. He pushed it back. He wanted to take his time with his mate. Leaving her lips, he moved to her ear. He swirled his tongue inside it before he took her earlobe between his teeth and gave it a tug. She shivered. With small nips, he trailed his mouth down the slim column of her throat. She grabbed the bottom of his t-shirt and pulled it up to his chest.

"You have way too many clothes on, Sef."

They both had too many clothes on for his liking. With a wave of his hand, he willed the clothes off their bodies. Chandra gasped as her skin came into sudden contact with his.

She took her bottom lip between her teeth and moaned. "That trick of yours sure comes in handy."

Chandra shifted lower on the blanket and then dragged her tongue along his chest. His cock jerked when laved across one of his flat nipples before she sucked the small bud into her mouth. With a slight push, she got him to lie on his back. Sef lifted his head as she moved farther down his body. She kissed a path along his abs. She straddled his legs and trailed a finger down his cock. Their gazes met. Holding it, she wrapped her fingers around the base of his shaft and licked it from base to tip. He growled softly and arched his hips.

She pulled her gaze away and gave his cock her full attention. She swirled her tongue around the head before she took it inside her mouth. Sef groaned at the feel of her hot mouth closing around him. He couldn't pull his gaze away from the sight of his thick shaft slipping in and out of her mouth as she sucked him deep inside. He grew even harder. If he let her pleasure him this way for too long, he'd come, but he didn't want to do that. He wanted to be buried to the hilt inside her wet pussy as he came.

Sef soon took Chandra by the arm and urged her to come up his body. He cupped her bottom and stopped her before she could impale herself on his hard shaft. Keeping his hold on her, he positioned her so she straddled his head with her glistening pussy hovering above his mouth. With a purr, he spread her folds and ran the flat of his tongue along the length of her pussy. His purrs grew louder as he circled her clit with the tip of his tongue, then sucked on it. She let out a keening moan. Her hips bucked against his mouth.

Just before she would have come, Sef wrapped an arm around her waist and flipped her onto her back. He spread her legs with one thigh, took hold of his cock and sheathed himself in her moist heat with one stroke. Chandra wrapped her legs around his waist and held on to his shoulders as he pulled back and then thrust back into her. Her inner walls gripped his shaft in a tight fist while he pumped between her legs. His pace increased as he rode her harder. Rubbing her clit with each stroke in, he pushed her into an orgasm. Her pussy clutched at his cock. He fought to stop himself from coming. The lion inside him wanted to take her as his mate.

Sef pulled out of Chandra, rolled her onto her stomach and urged her up onto her hands and knees. He licked up her spine and moved between her spread legs. With a cat growl, he nipped her shoulder. He entered her from behind. She was even tighter in that position. The lion wanted her fast and hard. Taking hold of her hips, he surged into her again and again as his climax built. She pushed back on him as his strokes grew faster. She moaned. He reached around her and found her clit. He rubbed it while he continued to thrust into her. It didn't take much to send her into another orgasm. He shoved into her once, twice, before he threw back his head, and with a lion's roar, his cock emptied itself inside her.

His breath sawed in and out of his lungs. Sef pulled out of Chandra's pussy. Before he collapsed onto the blanket, he wrapped an arm around her waist and took her down with him so she lay with her back pressed to his chest. He held her close, and pressed her shapely ass against his now flaccid cock.

Sef didn't know how he'd be able to leave Chandra when he had to return to the underworld. Even though he'd only known her for such a short period of time, he couldn't remember what his life had been like without her in it. She'd become a part of him. He was just about to ask her if she'd accept him as her mate when a male voice called her name from on the barn floor.

CHAPTER SIX

"Chandra, are you in here?"

At the sound of Bill calling her name, Chandra stiffened. "Shit, it's Bill," she whispered to Sef. To Bill, she called out, "I'm up in the hayloft. I'll be down in a minute."

She looked around for her clothes, but she couldn't see them anywhere. That was when she remembered Sef had done something to make them disappear.

Chandra looked at Sef, who appeared none too worried. In a hushed voice, she asked, "My clothes? Where are they?" With a wave of his hand, they appeared back on her body. "Stay here until I can get rid of Bill. He probably is here to check on you, the lion. I'll have to think up something to explain why there isn't one locked up in the kennel downstairs. I'm sure he's noticed it's empty by now."

Hoping Sef would do as she asked, Chandra stood and then headed down the stairs. Bill stood next to the empty kennel. He gave her a questioning look when she walked over to him.

"What happened to the lion? He's still okay I hope."

"He's fine. He's, ah…" Chandra had no idea what the hell to tell Bill that would sound in any way plausible. "He's, ah…" She noticed his attention suddenly become riveted on something behind her.

Chandra turned to see what it could be and swore under her breath. Sef, who'd shifted to his lion form, came down the hayloft stairs and padded over to her. Bill's eyes grew round as Sef sat beside her and then licked her fingers.

"Are you sure it's safe to have him roaming around out of his kennel, Chandra? He is a lion, after all." The older man kept looking between her and Sef.

"Oh, it's perfectly safe. He's just a big pussycat." Sef purred loudly and leaned against her leg as he looked up at her.

"He can purr. I always thought big cats couldn't."

"Apparently, this one can." Chandra jumped as Sef stood and stuck his nose between her legs. She pushed him away and glared down at him. She swore she could see laughter lurking in his gold eyes.

"Well, he seems to like you," Bill said with a laugh. "And I must say his wounds seem to have healed extraordinarily fast. You really must have a magic touch, Chandra."

"I don't know if I'd go that far, Bill. His wounds turned out not to be as nearly bad as they looked. His fur covers most of them."

"I'm glad to see he's doing better. So far, no one has reported a missing lion, which is damn strange in my opinion. He didn't just appear out of nowhere."

"You never know," Chandra said.

"He has to belong to somebody. Lions aren't exactly native to Ontario. Do you want me to start calling around to see if any zoos or wildlife parks would be willing to take him?"

"No!" Chandra cleared her throat, hoping to cover her

loud outburst. "I mean, no, that's okay. He can stay with me. I've grown kind of attached to him."

She had stronger feelings for Sef than just mere attachment, but she wasn't about to say that out loud in front of Bill. He didn't need to know she'd fallen for a shapeshifting Egyptian god. Or that somehow he'd wormed his way into her heart after such a short period of time.

"What if no one comes forward to claim him? You can't seriously think you can keep him indefinitely."

"Why not? It's not as if I don't have the room for him." Chandra looked down at Sef as she ran her fingers through his thick mane. Her next words were more for his benefit rather than Bill's. "It gets kind of lonely knocking around this big place on my own. He's more than welcome to stay with me. I'd miss him terribly if he left. If I have my way, I'd never let him go."

She pulled her gaze off Sef and looked back at Bill. He wore a confused expression. "Okay, if that's how you feel, Chandra, I'll leave the lion in your capable hands. I'll let Violet know he's doing much better, and about your decision to keep him. Just be careful."

"We'll be fine, Bill. Tell Violet I said hello."

Chandra waited until she heard Bill's car drive away before she focused her attention on the lion that stood at her side. "I thought I told you to stay up in the hayloft."

The lion's form wavered and blurred as Sef shifted to his human form. He wore the same jeans and t-shirt he had on earlier. "You had a hard time trying to come up with an excuse as to why your lion couldn't be found in his kennel. I thought if Bill saw me it'd make it easier for you."

"My lion?" Chandra stepped closer and wrapped her arms around his waist. "Are you my lion, Sef?"

Sef cupped her face in his large hands. "Yes. I'm your mate, Chandra. Will you accept me as yours?"

"Yes." She shook her head and smiled. "How can I have fallen for you so quickly, and so hard? I never believed in love at first sight, but it happened when I met you."

"It's because we're meant to be. You were meant to be mine." Sef kissed the tip of her nose.

"What happens now? You said so yourself that you have to return to the underworld. I can't be there with you, can I?"

"No, you can't. I'll think of some way to be with you, Chandra. And I want forever with you, not just one mortal lifetime. I don't have the power to make you an immortal like me. I can only take away the marks of death from the dead, but I'll ask one of the other gods to make you one."

Chandra shook at the implication of Sef's words. He wanted to make her immortal so they could be together forever. She'd thought herself lucky if she found a man who'd willingly commit a lifetime to her, but this Egyptian god wanted so much more. Going on tiptoe, she took his mouth in a slow, languid kiss.

Against his lips, she said, "I know I just had you, but take me to bed, Sef. I want to feel you inside me again."

With a cat growl, Sef lifted her against his chest and then carried her out of the barn. He somehow managed to open the front door of the house while he devoured her with his mouth. After kicking the door shut behind them, he took the stairs two at a time. Inside her bedroom, Chandra kicked off her shoes as he yanked the covers down to the bottom of the bed. He placed her onto the mattress and then only took the time to remove his own shoes before he followed her down.

Angling his head, Sef increased the pressure of his mouth on her lips. He reached up and cupped her breast through her shirt. Chandra moaned as he rubbed a thumb back and forth against her taut nipple.

Once he kissed along her jaw, she said in a breathy

voice, "Do what you did in the barn. Get rid of our clothes."

"Patience," Sef murmured against her skin. "I want to kiss every inch of you I bare, slowly."

Chandra groaned. "Are you trying to kill me?"

Sef chuckled. "My mate needs to learn how to be patient." He gave her bottom a smack, he lowered his head and bit her nipple through her shirt. Chandra gasped.

True to his word, Sef took his time removing her clothes. Shifting on the bed so he lay next to her, he pulled up her shirt and kissed every inch of skin he revealed. He drew lazy circles with his tongue. After he pulled it over her head, he undid the front clasp of her bra so it popped open. Chandra pulled the straps down her arms. With a rumbling growl, he bent his head and flicked each of her nipples with the tip of his tongue. Gently, he bit one, then sucked it deep into his mouth. Each pull caused ripples of pleasure inside her pussy.

He worked the button free on her jeans and then unzipped them. Sef pulled them down her legs and off. The feel of his tongue caressing her skin across her ribs, then down to her stomach had Chandra writhing on the bed. A large hand took hold of her hip and held her down. With his teeth, he pulled her panties down past her hips to her legs. She kicked them off. His lips blazed a trail across her hip bones and down to the tops of her thighs. She wanted to scream with frustration when he deliberately avoided her pussy — the one place where she wanted him to touch her the most.

When she would have grabbed Sef by the hair and put his mouth between her legs, he took her around the waist and flipped her onto her stomach. The sound of his purring filled the bedroom as he moved her hair aside and bit her where her neck and shoulder met. Chandra gasped at the pleasure/pain it gave her. He licked the spot.

He continued to make a trail of kisses across her back

and down. At her bottom, Sef gently bit each globe of flesh and spread her legs. He probed her slick opening with his fingers. Chandra moaned and arched her hips up off the mattress as she offered herself to him, needing a stronger touch. She moaned once two fingers were pushed past her folds and sunk deep inside her pussy. As Sef plunged them in and out of her core, she squeezed her inner muscles around them. It felt good, but she wanted his thick cock spearing her instead.

She would have rolled onto her back, but Sef pushed her back down. He shifted until he knelt between her spread thighs and sat back on his legs. With a hand on either side of her hips, he lifted her bottom into the air. Once he had her in position, he slipped the head of his cock into her wet pussy. Chandra tried to push back on him, to take more of him inside her, but he didn't allow it. His grip firm on her hips, he slowly rocked into her, not giving her any more of his length. She whimpered as she squeezed the muscles of her core into a tight fist around him.

Sef pulled free of her body, then pushed home in one stroke. Chandra moaned at the feel of him filling her to capacity. He was in so deep the head of his cock butted up against her cervix. He pulled back again before he surged into her again and again. With each hard thrust, her climax built. She held on to the sheet beneath her. His hips surged powerfully between her legs.

Suddenly, he pulled out of her and then flipped her onto her back. His cock slid back into her as he lay atop her with his weight rested on his elbows. He took her mouth in a hot kiss, his hips pistoning between her spread thighs. Once he had her clawing at his back, he slightly lifted his head and continued to move in her.

"Come for me, my mate. I want to feel that sweet pussy of yours clutch my cock as you come."

Chandra wrapped her legs around Sef's waist and

angled her hips so his hard shaft stroked her clit as it slid in and out of her. Then she was there. With a keening moan, she climaxed. Her pussy clutched his cock in a strangle hold and milked him. He lifted his upper body onto his hands and thrust into her. His pace quickened until he sank into her one final time and his climax claimed him. His cock pulsed deep inside her core as the liquid warmth of his cum filled her. He collapsed on top her. His much greater weight caused her to sink deeper into the mattress. She didn't care. She held him close and stroked his back. How would she ever be able to let him go?

CHAPTER SEVEN

They spent most of the day in bed making love. The only time they left Chandra's bedroom was when she had to take care of the animals in the barn, or she had to get herself something to eat. After she'd bedded down the animals for the night, she and Sef ended up in the shower where they made love again until the hot water ran out.

Now dressed in one of her large night shirts, Chandra sat on the couch cuddled up to Sef as they watched television. He wore a pair of pajama bottoms, which were an exact match to the ones he'd seen on a commercial. She had a feeling with him around she'd never have to worry about clothes shopping again.

Chandra had let Sef have the remote for the television. She showed him how to change the channels, and then let him go to town with it. So far, he'd already gone through all the channels three times.

"Can't find anything you want to watch?" she said as a smile played along her lips.

Sef stopped channel surfing and looked at her. "Sorry. There are too many choices."

"Why don't we watch this?"

Chandra took the remote from Sef and switched the channel to a movie she'd happened to catch a glimpse of before he'd changed it. It'd only started a few minutes before so they hadn't missed much of the beginning. She closely watched Sef as *The Mummy* played on the television screen. His gaze became glued to it as Brendan Fraser was chased by something deep in the sand at the ancient city of Hamunaptra in Egypt. Halfway through she went into the kitchen for something to drink. He'd continued to watch and had only nodded when she'd told him where she was going.

She flipped on the kitchen light and then headed to one of the cupboards. After taking out a glass, Chandra turned back around to get some water out of the cooler that stood in the corner next to the table. She let out a scream, and the glass fell out of her hand and smashed on the floor. A man stood in front of her. His eyes glowed an eerie red. She tried to get past him, but he quickly took hold of her arm in a bruising grip.

He pulled her close. "Where is the lion? Where is the guardian of the gate?"

A loud lion's roar of rage filled the kitchen. Chandra whimpered as the man held her in front of him and turned to face Sef, who stood just inside the room. His upper lip curled back as he growled menacingly at her attacker.

"Let my mate go, demon."

Chandra grew very still as a large knife appeared in the demon's hand. With her held against his chest as a shield, he raised it to her throat.

"If I'd known you'd find your mate in the mortal realm, I'd never have trapped you here. I thought you and your twin would find it hard to cope. I guessed wrong it would seem. All is not lost. I can put your mate to good use." Sef took a step closer. The demon shook his head and pressed the knife closer to Chandra's throat. She hissed as the sharp blade cut into her skin. "Don't come any closer, guardian. And don't even think of shifting to your lion form. She'll be dead before you get a chance to sink those vicious claws of yours into me."

Sef fisted his hands at his sides. "Where is my brother, demon? I know you trapped him here in the mortal realm with me."

The demon smiled evilly. "I see my spell worked. Not only did it work to trap you both, but it also stopped you from being able to communicate with each other. One of my men has gone to take care of your twin even as we speak. Soon I'll be rid of you both."

"We aren't that easy to kill, demon." Sef snarled.

"Maybe not, but your mate gives me an advantage over you. Mortals are so very easy to kill, so fragile. Just one cut of my knife, and she'll bleed to death in seconds."

Chandra whimpered with fear as the demon pushed the knife even closer. She felt a trickle of blood drip down her throat. She looked at Sef. The muscles in his arms bunched as he seemed to fight to keep himself from going on the attack. A tear slipped down her face as she realized he could do nothing to save her.

"If you hurt my mate, I'll shred you into pieces so small they won't be able to collect them all."

"Idle threats will get you nowhere, guardian. Enough of this chit chat. It's time to make yourself useful."

"I'll do nothing for you as long as you have my mate."

"And I won't let your mate go unless you do what I want. It'd seem we're at a bit of a standstill with your poor little mate stuck in the middle." Chandra cringed as the demon dragged his tongue along her cheek. "I can taste her fear on her skin. Nothing tastes sweeter than a mortal's fear."

Sef roared loudly. "I'll make you pay for that, demon. Just as I'll make you pay for spilling the blood of my mate."

"You will do nothing," the demon shot back. "As I said before, idle threats will get you nowhere. I've had more than enough of this."

The demon spoke in a language Chandra didn't recognize. As the words left his mouth, she felt an invisible power build around them. Sef stiffened. After the demon said the last words, the world disappeared beneath her feet. She yelled for Sef as she fell into darkness. The demon's grip on her never loosened, and they continued to fall.

Unable to see or sense Sef's presence with them, she panicked. One part of her hoped the demon had left him in the mortal realm, but another part of her hoped he'd taken Sef with them. Only with Sef did she stand a chance of getting away.

Solid ground suddenly rose to meet them. Chandra jolted against the demon and gasped with pain as the knife he'd somehow managed to keep at her throat cut deeper into her skin. After the darkness cleared, her panic subsided a little once she saw Sef. He stood in front of a large wooden door banded with metal.

Chandra looked around. They appeared to be in a cavern. Dark rock surrounded them on all sides and hung above their heads. The only light came from the two lit torches placed on either side of the door set into the rock. The door had to be the entrance to the underworld.

Chandra cried out when the demon grabbed a fistful of her hair and pulled her head back to better expose her throat. "Open the gate, guardian."

"And if I refuse?" Sef snarled.

"Then you'll be mated no more."

Chandra briefly closed her eyes and swallowed. She couldn't let the demon use her to make Sef open the gate to the underworld. She didn't know exactly what the demon would do once he was inside, but it didn't take much for her to figure it wouldn't be good. Desperately, she rolled her gaze in Sef's direction. All the muscles in his upper body stood out in stark relief as the light from the torches played across them. He held himself so stiffly she easily saw the thick veins in his arms. A steady growl rumbled out of his chest.

She shifted her gaze off Sef and frantically searched the cavern for something, anything, that could help her get free from the demon. She couldn't allow him to use her against Sef. Tears of frustration rose behind her eyes once she realized there was nothing she could use.

Her gaze landed back on Sef. The look of utter hopelessness she saw in his gold eyes shot straight through her. If she could be removed from the equation, he'd have no problem defeating the demon. As an immortal, he stood a better chance of survival than she did. And as one of the Egyptian gods who guarded the underworld, he had to be the one to walk away from this. No matter what happened, her life would be forfeit. The demon would kill her if Sef didn't open the gate, and if he did, the demon wouldn't just hand her back to her mate. That left Chandra with only one option.

Catching Sef's gaze, she looked at him with all the love she felt for him. Silently, she mouthed the words, *I love you*. Not wanting him to guess at what she intended to do, Chandra ignored the pain on her scalp where the demon held her and took a step forward. With a turn of her head, the sharp knife at her throat cut through her jugular vein like butter. As her life's blood quickly pumped out of her, she kept her gaze locked on to Sef. The sound of his roar of pain was the last thing she heard before everything went black.

*

Sef roared with uncontrollable rage as the demon dropped Chandra's lifeless body at his feet. He launched himself at the demon and shifted to his lion form in midair. The demon struck out at him with the sword that he now held in his hand. Sef didn't feel the pain as the sword cut across his chest. It couldn't compare to the one in his heart.

To have watched Chandra's blue eyes go dull and lifeless as her life ended hurt unlike anything he'd ever felt before. Mad with grief, he struck out at the demon with his razor-sharp claws. The need to render, to main, overtook him. Unable to get out of reach, the demon took hit after hit. Sef sank his claws into his legs and pulled him down. With a roar of triumph, he clamped his powerful jaws around the demon's throat and ripped it out.

Slowly Sef backed away from the demon's body. Blood dripped from his muzzle and from the wounds he'd received during the fight. Numb to the pain, he turned back to where Chandra lay. He shifted to human form and dropped to the ground beside her. He gathered her lifeless body into his arms and roared. It wasn't fair. He'd only just found her. Tears that he'd never shed before in his very long life fell.

He brushed Chandra's blonde hair aside. Her face already felt cold to the touch. Seeing the gaping wound in her throat, he placed his hand on it and used his power to heal it. If only he could so easily restore her life.

Angry over his inability to bring Chandra back to him, Sef called out to Ra. "Ra! My brother and I have served you faithfully for centuries. I've never asked you for anything until now. Give me my mate back. She gave up her life to keep demon kind from entering the underworld. That has to mean something to you."

At first, Sef didn't think Ra would answer him. Then the sun god's voice filled his head.

I feel your pain, Sef. If I give your mate back her life, I won't release you from your duty as the guardian to the underworld. And your mate can't dwell here with you.

Sef brushed a kiss across Chandra's cold brow. "If I must give her up so she can live, I'll gladly do it."

I wouldn't ask that of you, Sef. You'll be able to be with your mate during the day, but at night you must return to guard the gate.

"As long as I can be with Chandra. That's all that matters."

Then I give your mate back her life, and immortality. Tonight you may stay with her, but tomorrow night I expect you to return to your duties.

As Chandra tool her first breath, Sef silently thanked Ra. Once she blinked up at him, he flashed them to her house in the mortal realm. In seconds, he had her inside her bedroom. She looked at him as he placed her on her feet and then stripped her of her bloodstained night shirt.

"How can this be, Sef? I died."

Shaking with emotion, Sef willed his pajama bottoms off his body and pulled Chandra close. "Ra gave you back your life. He also made you immortal. We have forever to be together now."

Chandra went on her tiptoes and kissed him. "Take me to bed, Sef," she said against his mouth. "I need you to hold me close."

Sef picked Chandra up into his arms and gently then placed her onto the bed. He followed her down, and she wrapped her arms around his neck and kissed him thoroughly.

As he slid inside her, he lifted his head, and said, "I love you, Chandra. I'll never let you go."

Chandra caressed his cheek. "I love you too, my Egyptian god."

As he moved inside her, Sef knew nothing would ever separate them again. Not even death.

The End

DUAU, LION OF TOMORROW

Unable to shift out of lion form, Duau is stuck in the mortal realm, separated from his twin brother, Sef. Weak from wounds received in battle with the demons who'd trapped him, he finds help in the form of the mortal woman who takes him in as a lion.

Darcie takes the wounded lion into her home against her better judgment. After he shifts into human form and tells her he's an Egyptian god, she falls for the immortal she has taken in. Can an immortal ever come to love a mortal?

Stuck in the mortal realm and unable to find his twin, Duau knows Darcie is his mate, but she'd never survive the underworld where he must return. Can he give up the mortal woman who has his heart, or will he be the death of her?

CHAPTER ONE

Duau shifted to his lion form just as his twin brother, Sef, shifted to his. He eyed the group of demons who stood before them. The demons wanted into the underworld. It was his and Sef's job to make sure they didn't get past the gate. They each guarded one where the sun god Ra entered and exited each night to make sure demon kind stayed out.

With a signal from their leader, the demons drew their swords. Duau growled as he caught sight of Sef bunching his powerful back legs under him as he prepared for the attack. As Barbary lions, they could easily take down the demons with their razor-sharp claws and teeth. That they both weighed six hundred pounds of solid muscle gave them a bit of an advantage as well. When they hit the demons, they'd hit them hard.

Sef launched himself at the closest demon with a roar. Duau did the same. He brought the demon down and sank his claws in deep as he ripped out his throat. Quickly, he turned to face his next opponent. Slowly, the demons fell one at a time until only their leader remained. Duau circled around him to one side as Sef took the other. Duau ignored the pain from the wounds he'd received, especially the wicked sword cut he'd taken across the chest, and hemmed the demon in.

The demon's eyes glowed red once they stalked closer. "You may have defeated the others, but I get the last strike."

With his hands raised in their direction, the demon somehow pinned them in place. Duau roared as he fought the hold over him. Sef roared as well as he fought to break free. The demon laughed at their futile attempts at freedom. He recited a spell, and a chill ran down Duau's spine. Once the demon completed it, he and Sef would be trapped in the mortal realm, separated from each other. Duau had only enough time to catch his twin's gaze before they were yanked from the underworld.

* * * *

Darcie Clark pushed open the sliding glass door and then stepped out onto her back deck. With a large mug of steaming hot tea in her hand, she went and sat at the patio table. She took a sip of her drink and she looked out across the lake. In places she saw some of the early morning mist that still hung above the water yet to be burned off by the sun. The trees along the edge had already turned now that fall had arrived, their leaves ranging from rich reds to a burnished gold.

She loved this time of year because of the colors. It'd also been one of the reasons she'd decided to move up north to the heart of Ontario's cottage country after her divorce. Living on the shores of a lake in Muskoka, Darcie couldn't have asked for anything more. As an artist, the lake and surrounding woods gave her more than enough inspiration to paint.

Darcie lifted her face to the sun, closed her eyes and took a deep breath. *Today I'll paint outside*, she thought. The days that she could work outdoors were numbered. All too soon winter would arrive, and she'd be relegated to the house to paint. Winters in Muskoka tended to be a little colder and snowier than what she'd had to contend with when she lived in Toronto, but she could handle it. Summer and fall more than made up for it.

She lifted her mug to take another sip of tea. A noise coming from the woods at the side of her house drew her attention. Darcie put her mug down onto the patio table and went to stand at the railing that faced the woods. With a hand held to her forehead to shade her eyes from the glare of the sun, she looked through the trees to see what could have made the noise. She couldn't find anything. The noise, a cross between a grunt and a growl, came a second time. Curious as to what made the sound, she crossed to the stairs that led to the lawn below.

Darcie pulled the thick sweater she wore closer around her and headed to the wooded area next to her house. As soon as she stepped into the trees, she noticed the slight drop in temperature. The sun hadn't risen high enough yet to penetrate the thick foliage. Carefully, she picked a path, stepping over fallen branches and logs. She stopped when she heard the noise again. It came from a spot a couple yards away directly in front of her.

Cautiously, Darcie approached the large fallen tree. Once she came close enough, she peered over it. Her heart jumped into her throat at what she saw lying on the ground on the other side. A huge male lion lay stretched out with its head on its front paws. He made the grunt/growl sound as he tried to heave himself up. She quickly took note of the blood that marred his fur. He obviously was injured, but she didn't plan to stick around to see to what extent.

She took a step back with the hopes she could slip away before he became aware of her presence. Once she was safely inside the house, she'd call someone who knew how to handle wild animals and have them get the lion. Darcie couldn't imagine how he'd ended up in her woods.

The loud sound of a branch breaking echoed through the tress as Darcie took another step back. She stiffened. The lion's head shot up and turned in her direction. His gold-eyed gaze locked on to her as he clumsily lurched to his feet.

"Oh, shit, oh shit, oh shit," Darcie said out loud. She quickly spun around and took off at a run.

She wended her way through the trees, and looked back once over her shoulder in time to see the lion jump over the fallen tree in one bound. Darcie heard him coming up behind her. He closed the distance between them too quickly for her liking. Once she reached the spot where her lawn began, she put on an extra burst of speed. She just needed to get inside the house before he caught up with her.

Thinking herself home free after she reached the stairs that led up to the deck, Darcie raced up them two at a time. Just as she stepped onto the deck something big and heavy slammed into the back of her. She went down hard onto her hands and knees. A large paw hooked her by the shoulder and flipped her onto her back. She dug her heels into the wooden deck and tried to inch away from the lion that now stood above her. A small whimper of fear escaped her lips when he put a front paw on her stomach. She instantly went still.

The lion went to stand over her, straddling her. He stuck his nose into the crook of her neck and sniffed. Darcie flinched. He dragged his raspy tongue along her skin. She held her breath and waited for him to sink his sharp teeth into her next. The air left her lungs in a *whoosh* as he licked her again and then lifted his head to look her right in the eyes.

Darcie tried to pull her gaze away, but found she couldn't. The lion's gold one trapped her attention. The fear she felt slowly slipped away. She knew he wouldn't hurt her. She suddenly felt the overwhelming need to get the lion inside her house. She was crazy to even think it, but it was something she couldn't say no to.

The lion's back legs suddenly crumpled beneath him, and he landed on top her. Darcie lifted the big head that rested on her chest. The lion's eyes were closed. She placed her hand on his chest, then breathed a sigh of relief. His heart beat strong beneath it. When she pulled away, her palm came away coated with the lion's blood. Alarmed by the sight of so much of it, she quickly worked her way out from under his prone body. Obviously, he'd passed out from his wounds.

Darcie looked down at her sweater and found it had blood on it. She really needed to get the lion inside so she could look after his wounds. It was more of a compulsion than anything. Not that she could really do anything more than clean them up and somehow bandage them.

Knowing she couldn't just pick the lion up and carry him inside, she looked from him to the sliding glass patio door. How the hell would she manage on her own to get a full-grown male lion that had to weigh a ton into the house? Only one idea came to mind—she'd have to drag him inside.

Not wasting any more time, Darcie rushed inside and got an old quilt out of the upstairs linen closet. Back outside, she spread it out on the deck next to the lion, and as gently as she could, she rolled him onto it. Then came the hard part of actually moving him into the house. She took hold of an end of the quilt and pulled with all her might. She managed to move him an inch.

Determined to succeed, she slowly dragged the lion up to the sliding glass door. Out of breath, Darcie sat on the deck next to him. Sweat poured off her. Decidedly overheated, she yanked off her sweater and then chucked it through the open door. Once she caught her breath, she stood and took hold of the quilt at the lion's head. She grunted with the strain as she maneuvered him so he laid half in and half out the door. With another big heave, she pulled him the rest of the way inside.

He was still out cold, but he'd wake up at some point. She may be crazy to want to bring him inside her house, but she wasn't that crazy to think she'd let him wander around unrestrained. She raced upstairs before she snagged one of her wide leather belts and then brought it to the living room where the lion lay. Next, she went outside to her detached garage and got the thick length of chain the previous owners had left behind. With her belt acting as a collar, she looped the chain through it and put it around the lion's neck. She attached the length of chain to her sturdy solid oak banister.

Satisfied that the chain would hold him, at least she hoped it would, Darcie grabbed some clean towels before she set to work on the lion's wounds. The one on his chest looked to be the worst of the bunch. She used an old sheet, which she ripped into strips, and tied them around his chest and back.

Feeling as if she'd spent an hour working out at the gym, Darcie stood and stretched her sore back. She caught sight of her clothes and grimaced. She'd done all she could for the lion. What she'd do with him once he woke up, she'd deal with it when the time came. For now, a shower was in order. After one last look at the lion, she went upstairs to clean up.

CHAPTER TWO

Duau slowly came out of the darkness that had claimed him. Disoriented and weak, he looked around at his surroundings. He had no idea how he'd come to be there. The last thing he remembered was chasing the mortal woman who'd found him in the woods, of staring into her hazel eyes as he placed the idea of allowing him into her house inside her mind. Then all had gone black.

He shook his head and heard the rattle of a chain. He felt the weight of it that hung at his neck. Duau let out a grunt. The woman had not only brought him inside her home after he'd passed out, she'd also chained him to the banister attached to the stairs that led to the upper level. She hadn't completely trusted him, after all. He could understand her wanting to be cautious of him.

Painfully, Duau pulled himself up on all four paws. His wounds had already begun to heal, but the deep sword thrust he'd taken during the battle with the demons would take longer. It left him weak. With the need to find out exactly where he was, he tried to shift to his human form. A shiver of unease shot through him when he realized his weakness prevented him from making the change. It also made him think of Sef and where his twin could be.

Duau knew for a fact the demon had made sure to separate them once they'd arrived in the mortal realm. He telepathically called out to Sef, hoping his twin would hear him. Sef didn't answer, nor did he answer after he tried a second and then a third time. His unease increased. Desperately, Duau tried to make the change once again. His loud roar of frustration reverberated off the walls inside the room. In response, there was the sound of hurried footsteps from the floor above him.

Duau's breath caught in his lungs as the mortal woman hurriedly came down the stairs with only a towel wrapped around her. She held it in place with a hand at her chest. Her damp long, black hair hung down to the middle of her back. He took a deep breath in as she stepped cautiously closer. The lion part of him roared as the scent of his mate filled his head. And this woman *was* his mate. He'd known it when he'd stood above her outside and her scent had washed over him. He hadn't been able to resist tasting her skin. It made him hungry to taste the rest of her body, especially the place between her slim thighs.

"You're awake," she said as she came to stand in front of him.

He sensed her uncertainty. She half reached out to touch him, but pulled her hand back at the last minute. His roar must have scared her. Not wanting his mate to be afraid of him, Duau stretched his head out as far as the chain would allow and purred once he managed to come in contact with her fingers. With each breath he took, the sound of his purrs filled the room. The woman came a little closer and allowed him to swirl his tongue around her fingertips. She smiled down at him. He saw a flash of her thigh through the slit in the towel. Unable to resist, he shoved his face through it and tried to lick the seam of her pussy with his raspy tongue. The woman let out a little shriek of surprise and pushed him away.

"I see I'm going to have to watch you," she said with a smile that tugged at her lips. "I may be thirty-five and divorced with no boyfriend, but that doesn't mean I'm desperate."

Duau grunted, happy to hear his mate had no other ties to another male. Not that another man in her life would stop him from claiming her as his mate once he could shift to his human form. The one quick almost taste between her legs had him longing for more. He couldn't wait to get her beneath him as he sank his cock into her pussy.

The woman backed away slightly as Duau swept his hungry gaze up her slim body. "You better not be sizing me up to see how many bites it'll take to eat me."

Duau didn't hold back the purr that rose inside him. Oh, he'd be eating her, just not the way she thought. He'd feast on her pussy until she came against his mouth.

She sighed and shook her head. "You're losing it, Darcie. First you take a wild animal into your home and now you're talking to him as if he understands you." She turned around and headed for the stairs. With a quick look over her shoulder, she said, "I'll get dressed and be back down in a few minutes. Be a good lion and try not to tear apart anything before I come back."

As she walked up the stairs, Duau followed her with his gaze until he could no longer see her shapely calves. He settled back down onto the floor. He needed to rest. Once he felt strong again, he'd make the change and claim her as his mate. He couldn't wait.

* * * *

Darcie ran a comb through her damp hair, then pulled on the pair of old sweat pants and t-shirt she wore when she painted. She went back downstairs after that. The lion lifted his head off his paws where he lay on the floor once she reached the bottom step. He really was a beautiful cat. His gold-eyed gaze followed her as she went to stand a short distance away. She'd have to keep an eye on him. He'd completely caught her off guard earlier when he'd shoved his head between her legs and tried to lick her pussy. What bothered her most about it was how that one almost stroke of the lion's tongue made her feel. It'd felt good, too good for her peace of mind. That alone told her she'd gone too long without a man in her bed. That a lion could turn her on with what would have been an innocent lick really showed how low she'd sunk.

She crossed her arms across her chest and stared down at the lion. She'd planned on painting outside today, but she didn't want to leave him alone inside her house. If he decided to tear into her hardwood floors, or any furniture he could get in reach of with his razor-sharp claws, she wanted to be around to somehow stop him. She didn't know exactly what she would do, but she would come up with something if she needed to. Her gaze swept the lion from the top of his head to the tip of his tail. She knew exactly what she'd do today — paint his portrait. The chance of having a wild animal such as he this close for her to paint wouldn't happen again. She didn't do many animal paintings, she mostly did landscapes, but she couldn't pass up on this opportunity.

Darcie went to the corner of the room where her easel stood folded. She set it up near the lion, making sure it stayed out of his reach. Next, she got a blank canvas and then moved the small table that held all her painting supplies beside the easel.

She picked up her charcoal pencil and turned back to study the lion before she sketched on the canvas. "Okay, handsome, you just lay there and I'm going to paint you."

The lion cocked his head in her direction when she spoke. Darcie smiled, then soon became lost in her work as she sketched. It didn't take her very long to get the charcoal outline of the lion onto the canvas. Once finished that, she mixed paints together on her palette until she had the gold of his eyes and the blond and dark brown color of his mane perfect. She picked up a paintbrush and set to work.

As always when she painted, the rest of the world fell away, leaving only the canvas in front of her and what she painted as her sole focus. Sometimes it lasted a few hours or the whole day. Lost in her painting, Darcie would at times be shocked to find the number of hours she'd actually worked when she finally came out of it.

Her ability to shut everyone out had been too much for her now ex-husband to handle. After her paintings garnered interest and then made some sales through a gallery in Toronto, he'd become pissed off with the number of hours she spent working. He'd complained that she never paid any attention to him. At the end of their marriage, he'd given her the ultimatum to either stop painting or lose him. When he'd said he'd put up with her hobby, as he called her painting, and that he wanted her pregnant within a month as if she were some brood mare, Darcie knew what her decision would be. She couldn't stay married to a man who'd force her to give up her dreams.

The hours flew by as the image of the lion took shape on her canvas. Much to Darcie's surprise he made a very good subject. He held his position for the most part, only moving his head back down to his paws when he went to sleep for a couple hours. After he woke up, she felt his gaze intently watching her as she worked.

Late in the afternoon, Darcie put her paintbrush into a jar of turpentine to soak and then stepped away from her easel. She put her arms over her head and stretched her back and shoulders. Pleased with what she'd accomplished, she put the easel back in the corner, leaving the canvas on it to dry. Once she had the small table put back as well, she turned to the lion. He still watched her. It suddenly hit her that she hadn't thought to give him anything to eat or drink since he'd awakened the first time.

Darcie looked down at her paint-stained hands. She would have to clean up first. Turning her attention back to the lion, she said, "Sorry about that, handsome. I should have given you some water, at least, to drink. Just give me a few minutes to clean the paint off my hands and then I'll get you some. I'll also try to scrounge up something for you to eat."

Before she could step away, the lion stood. Her brows furrowed as his body blurred and wavered. Between one heartbeat and the next, a man stood in the lion's place. And not just any ordinary man. Darcie had to stop her jaw from dropping open as her gaze skimmed over him from head to toe. He was beyond gorgeous with his chest bare, except for her makeshift bandages, with only a snow-white ancient Egyptian-looking linen kilt worn low on his hips. She had to tilt her head up to look him in the face. She guessed his height to be six-foot-ten, which towered over her five-foot-six. His dark brown hair touched his shoulders. As she met his gaze, she noticed his eyes were the same gold color of the lion's. She looked at his sculpted lips and swallowed.

Reluctantly, she pulled her gaze away from his sinful-looking mouth and met his gaze once more. "Ah...what...who?"

She sounded like a brainless idiot, unable to string a coherent thought together, but how else should she act? She'd just watched a lion shift into a gorgeous hunk of a man. A man she suddenly wanted to screw until neither one of them could walk.

He smiled and swept his gaze to her breasts. Darcie's nipples pebbled beneath her t-shirt, the points pushing against the material. His smile widened as he lifted his gaze back up to her face.

"I'm Duau." He reached behind his neck and pulled off the belt that she'd put on the lion. He let it and the chain attached to it drop to the floor with a *thud*. He came to stand in front of her. His nostrils flared with his deep breath.

Darcie swallowed again at the hunger in Duau's gold eyes, the same look he'd given her earlier when in his lion form. "What are you?"

"I'm an Egyptian god. My twin brother, Sef, and I are the two halves of the Egyptian god Aker, the guardian of the gates to the underworld. I'm also your mate. As for your offer of food and water, I don't require anything, except for maybe a taste of your sex, preferably as you come against my mouth." Duau stepped closer so his chest touched the tips of Darcie's suddenly aching breasts.

Maybe it was because she hadn't eaten anything all day, or because Duau overwhelmed all her senses, but whatever the cause, Darcie's world spun just before she collapsed against him in a dead faint.

CHAPTER THREE

Duau easily caught Darcie as she slumped against him. He shifted her until he lifted her into his arms. With her cradled against his chest, he went to the couch and then laid her on it. He stretched out next to her with her body tucked up against him. He trailed a finger down her soft cheek and shook his head. Her fainting hadn't been what he'd expected her to do once he shifted to his human form.

Lowering his head, Duau brushed his lips gently across hers. "Darcie. Wake up, my mate."

She stirred against him and her eyes blinked open. She looked around before she focused on his face. "I fainted." Darcie said it as a statement, not a question. "I've never fainted before in my life."

Duau brushed a lock of hair off her forehead. "That may have been my fault. I think seeing me shift out of my lion form may have shocked you."

"Well, it's not every day a girl gets to meet an Egyptian god who can shapeshift into a lion. I think it'd be a bit of a shock to anyone."

"I'll have to make it up to you."

Duau dipped his head once again and took Darcie's lips in a slow kiss. She stiffened against him, but as he slanted his mouth against hers, sweeping the seam of her lips with his tongue, she slowly relaxed. He pushed his way inside her mouth and swirled his tongue inside its heated depths for his first real taste of his mate. Once she kissed him back, he couldn't stop the purr that built inside him. The feel of her hands on his skin as they skimmed up his chest to clutch his shoulders had the lion inside him roaring with triumph.

He increased the pressure of his lips and sucked her tongue inside his mouth. She moaned. He rocked the hard length of his cock against her hip. He wanted to taste every inch of her skin, but he wouldn't have the patience to wait to take her. After waiting centuries to find his mate, and with the lion riding him to claim her as his, Duau wanted her hard and fast. Later he'd take the time to slowly make love to her, to learn every inch of her body with his lips and tongue.

His purrs filled the room. He grabbed the bottom of her shirt and pulled it over her head. He looked down at her breasts. Her taut nipples could be easily seen through the sheer pink lace material that covered them. Hooking a finger in the top of one lacy cup, Duau pulled it down until her rose-colored nipple popped free. With the tip of his tongue, he circled the taut peak. He continued it until Darcie slightly lifted her chest off the couch, offering him more. With a low growl that rumbled out of his chest, he opened his mouth and sucked her nipple deep inside. She moaned and threaded her fingers through his hair to hold him to her.

Duau lifted his head. He eyed the material that covered Darcie's breasts. As if she sensed his hesitation, she reached between her breasts and undid the front clasp. With her breasts now bared, he swooped down and sucked the other nipple into his mouth. He drew on the tight peak and stroked a hand down her side to the waistband of her pants. With a yank, he pulled them down past her hips and legs. She kicked them the rest of the way off.

After releasing her nipple with a small *pop,* Duau nuzzled her neck and pulled her panties off. He dipped his hand between Darcie's legs and growled with approval at the slick wetness he found there. He pushed one finger and then another inside her pussy. Her strong inner muscles squeezed around them as he slowly slid them in and out of her. She lifted her hips off the couch as she rode his fingers. His cock throbbed in anticipation of being buried deep inside her warm wet pussy. Unable to wait any longer, he quickly yanked off his kilt and the loincloth he wore beneath it. He moved to lie between her legs with the tip of his cock pressed against her slick folds.

Propped up on his elbows, he held most of his weight off Darcie. He held himself there, unmoving, until she opened her eyes and looked up at him. "I'm going to make you mine now. I'm going to sink my cock so deep inside you that you won't know where you end and I begin."

Darcie took her bottom lip between her teeth and moaned. She pressed her pussy down onto the head of his thick cock. "I can't believe I'm doing this, but god I want you."

Duau cupped Darcie's bottom in his hands and lifted her hips as he positioned himself. With one stroke, he seated his cock to the hilt inside her. He moaned at the feel of her tight pussy wrapped around his shaft. He pulled back and then slowly pushed every inch of him back into her. Darcie hooked her legs around his waist while he pumped his hips between her spread thighs.

His orgasm built. Duau pushed it back as he rode Darcie harder and increased his pace. He wanted her to come first, wanted her pussy clutching his cock in a tight fist as she came. Angling his hips at just the right angle, he rubbed his thick shaft against her clit and stroked faster.

Darcie's fingernails bit into his shoulders and she moaned. "Come for me, Darcie."

"I'm almost there," Darcie gasped. "Harder, Duau. Harder."

With a growl, Duau pounded into her. The inner walls of her core flexed around his cock. He continued to thrust into Darcie's pussy, then she fell over the edge. She gasped and moaned, and her pussy squeezed and released his shaft with her climax. Lifting her hips higher, he rode her hard and fast until he exploded deep inside her, filling her with his cum.

He dropped his head to her shoulder and fought to catch his breath. Darcie's arms came around him and held him close. Once he could breathe evenly again, Duau looked down at her. Her eyes fluttered open.

"Don't go to sleep. Making love to you once has hardly sated my hunger for you." Still semi-aroused, even though he'd come, Duau flexed his hips into her to show her he'd want her again very soon.

A small moan slipped past Darcie's lips. "Then you better let me up to eat. Unlike you, I need food to keep my energy up."

Reluctantly, Duau pulled free of her body and then slipped off the couch. Darcie's gaze raked over his body. His cock jerked as she stared at it with hunger in her eyes. "I suggest you not look at me like that or you won't be getting off that couch any time soon."

Darcie stood and then picked up her clothes that lay on the floor where he'd thrown them. "Don't go anywhere. I'll be back down in a minute."

Duau smiled as his mate disappeared up the stairs. He had no intentions of leaving, even if he could have left.

* * * *

Darcie grabbed her bathrobe out of her bedroom closet before she went to the bathroom. After she used the toilet, she snagged one of the clean cloths off the shelf and used it to clean herself. She grabbed another one in case Duau wanted to use one as well. Before she left the bathroom, she looked at her reflection in the mirror. The woman who stared back at her looked as if she'd been well loved. Her lips were still puffy from his kisses. Her cheeks had a pink flush. She reached up to straighten her mussed hair, but stopped when she noticed the dried paint on her hands. After turning back on the water, she washed them until all the paint was removed.

Before she went downstairs, she gave herself one last look-over. She still couldn't believe she'd actually fainted and then made love with Duau. It wasn't as if she slept around, and she sure as hell never slept with a man she'd just met. With Duau, she couldn't have refused him even if she'd wanted to. Yes, she found him extremely attractive, but it was more than just attraction. It just felt right to be with him. As if he was her missing half. Could she really be his mate as he'd called her? Hell if she knew. Right now, she'd take what she could and see what would happen tomorrow.

After snatching up the clean cloth, Darcie headed down to join Duau. He waited near the couch where she'd left him, still gloriously naked, except for the makeshift bandage across the center of his chest. Unable to stop herself, she looked down at his large cock, which stood semi-erect. She dragged her gaze away and walked over to him.

She offered Duau the cloth. "There's a washroom near the front door if you want to clean up. There's a shower upstairs, but I don't know if you want to be showering with that wound in your chest."

Duau looked down and ripped the bandage off before she could protest. Much to her surprise the wound looked almost healed. Only a slight red mark showed where the open wound had been. She also noticed his other wounds were gone. If she'd needed proof of his immortality, she had it now in how fast he healed.

He took the cloth she held out to him. "We both can take a bath later." He gave her a look that promised she'd more than enjoy it. "I'll make do with the washcloth for now."

As Duau turned around and headed for the washroom, Darcie hungrily watched his hard backside flex with each of his steps. The man didn't have an inch of fat on him anywhere. His body bulged with muscle. Knowing she could touch and it made her pussy ache to have that big cock of his deep inside it. She gave herself a mental shake, dragged her mind out of the gutter and headed for the kitchen to make something quick to eat. If she wanted to keep up with Duau, she'd need all the energy she could get.

CHAPTER FOUR

B y the time Duau returned from using the washroom, Darcie had heated up some leftovers she'd found in the fridge in the microwave. He walked into the kitchen completely at ease with his nakedness. Not bothering to sit at the kitchen table, she stood at the counter to eat. He came to stand in front of her.

In between a mouthful, Darcie asked, "How did you end up here, Duau? Muskoka, Ontario, isn't exactly close to Egypt."

Duau's face grew serious. "My brother, Sef, and I did battle with a group of demons who wanted into the underworld. We defeated them all, except for their leader. Before we could take him down, he used a spell to trap us in the mortal realm. He separated us as well."

"So you can't return to the underworld?"

"No, I can't. That doesn't bother me as much as my inability to contact Sef. We've always been able to talk to one another telepathically. I can't now. He hasn't answered my calls."

"I see." A small thrill shot through Darcie at the

thought of Duau being unable to go home yet. It was a bit selfish on her part, but she wanted time to get to know this Egyptian god better. "Would Sef be in his lion form as you were when I found you?"

"Yes. We both prefer to fight with claws and teeth instead of a sword. Already wounded, the demon's spell weakened me so I couldn't shift to human form until now. I would assume Sef would be unable to shift as well."

Darcie saw the worry Duau felt for his brother as his brows drew together in concern. "Hopefully, the demon sent Sef to a less-populated area as he did you. I hate to think what would happen to him if he ended up in the middle of downtown Toronto."

Finished with her quick meal, Darcie turned away and rinsed her plate in the sink before she put it into the dishwasher. She turned back around to find Duau had moved up behind her. Her pussy clenched as he looked down at her with hunger in his gold eyes. No man had ever gazed at her like that, not even her ex. Duau stared at her as if he wanted to devour her.

Duau undid the belt on her bathrobe and then pushed it open. "It's time to continue what we started on the couch."

Darcie met his lips halfway once Duau bent his head to take her mouth. His tongue stroked hers, and he pulled her against his hard body. His erection throbbed against her stomach. She feverishly kissed him back when he cupped her breast and stroked his thumb across her taut nipple. With her hands locked behind his neck, she pushed herself closer and moaned. Wetness pooled between her legs, and her pussy readied itself for his cock.

She trailed one hand down to his broad shoulder, then across his wide chest. She brushed her fingers over one flat nipple on her way down to Duau's washboard abs. After skimming down the rippled muscles of his stomach, she reached down and took his fully engorged cock in her hand. He was a big man in every sense of the word. He moaned against her mouth. She slowly pumped her hand up and down his hard length. He felt like velvet wrapped steel. Darcie knew how good it felt to have his cock buried to the hilt inside her. Her pussy wept, her juices running down her inner thighs.

Duau pulled her hand away, then lifted her so she sat on the counter in front of him. Shifting his lips to the side of her neck, he said in a thick voice, "I going to taste every inch of your skin."

Darcie shifted closer, and Duau licked a trail from her neck to her breast. He dragged his teeth along the tight peak before he sucked it inside his mouth. He paid equal attention to her other nipple until she squirmed against him. With a loud purr, he continued to make his way down her body. He swirled his tongue inside her bellybutton. She held on to the edge of the counter as he sank to his knees between her legs.

He caressed her inner thighs and spread them farther apart. Looking down, Darcie's breath caught in her throat at the sight of his head between her legs. She gripped the counter tighter. His tongue came out and flicked against her clit. Duau's purrs filled the kitchen when he lapped at her pussy, spreading her folds so he could spear his tongue inside her core. Oral sex had never done anything for her when her ex had gone down on her, but as he sucked and licked at her pussy, an orgasm built. She panted as he sucked her clit. She bucked her hips against his mouth when he pushed two fingers inside her, sliding them in and out. Unable to look away, she watched him pleasure her as she tightened around his fingers. Then she was there. With a moan, she let her head fall back as an intense orgasm tore through her.

Duau rose between her legs. Darcie's gaze fell to his fully erect cock. A bead of moisture sat on the very tip. With a finger, she reached out and rubbed it around the head. He groaned. He pulled her hips closer and then plunged his thick shaft inside her pussy with one stroke. She held on to his shoulders as he pulled back and then thrust into her once again. The feel of him rubbing against her clit had another climax quickly building inside her. She tunneled her fingers through his hair and took his mouth in a hot kiss. She sucked on his tongue and squeezed her inner muscles around his plunging cock. He put his hands on the counter on either side of her hips and pumped between her legs. Once she climaxed, fisting around his hard shaft, he pulled away from her mouth and let out a lion's roar. A second later, his cock pulsed inside her as he came.

Darcie let her head fall against Duau's shoulder as her breath rasped in and out of her lungs. "I think you're going to kill me, but it wouldn't be a bad way to go."

"I've only just begun to make love to you, my mate. I don't think I'll ever get enough of you." Duau picked her up off the counter and then headed for the stairs. His flaccid sex slipped free of her body as he took the steps two at a time. "I'll let you sleep for a little while before I take you again. I can't have my mate falling asleep on me while I love her."

Once inside her bedroom, he took off her bathrobe and put her into the bed. He slipped in beside her. Duau pulled her close so her head lay cushioned on his wide chest. Darcie felt relaxed and contented just to be held in his strong arms.

She drew lazy circles with her finger along his chest. "You keep calling me your mate."

"Because you are my mate."

Darcie tilted her head back so she could look up at him. "How can you know I am? You don't know anything about me."

"One whiff of your scent and I knew you were meant for me."

"And that's all that matters? That I smelled right to

you?"

Duau chuckled. "You sound as if you don't believe me."

"Well, I'll admit I can't find anything wrong with the sex, but I've already been married once, and that didn't work out that great."

A loud growl rumbled in her ear. "You're mine now. Even if you still belonged to another, I'd have claimed you as mine."

There was possessiveness in Duau's voice. He truly would have taken her away from her ex-husband if she was still married to him. She snuggled closer and let her eyes flutter shut. She wanted to believe she could keep Duau as her own, but Darcie didn't know how a mortal and an immortal Egyptian god could make it work. For now, she didn't want to think about it. She'd take what she could get. Tomorrow was always another day.

CHAPTER FIVE

Darcie awoke the next morning aching in places her body hadn't ached in quite some time. A smile spread across her face as she thought of the number of times she and Duau had made love during the night. He'd taken her in every position possible. They'd even made love in the shower at one point. He had stamina that just wouldn't quit.

She reached across the bed and found the spot next to her empty. With a frown, she pushed herself up on one elbow and looked around the room. She was alone. Had Duau somehow managed to return to the underworld while she'd slept? The thought that he'd already left had Darcie quickly getting out of bed. She picked up her bathrobe that still lay on the floor and then pulled it on. She didn't want to admit how panicky she felt as she rushed out of the room and headed downstairs. She didn't want to let him go just yet. During the night she'd come to accept him as her mate, the other half of herself. For someone who never thought to love again, she'd fallen head over heels for a man she may or may not be able to keep as her own.

Once on the lower level, Darcie's heart dropped when she couldn't see Duau in the living room or in the kitchen. "Duau?" She hated the sound of desperation she heard in her voice. "Duau, where are you?" she called out a little louder.

The sliding glass door that led out to her back deck opened, and Duau quickly stepped inside the house. His gaze shot around the room. "What's the matter? Are you all right?" He came over to her and placed his hands on her shoulders. He searched her face with his gaze.

Darcie shook her head and took a deep breath. "Nothing is the matter. It's just...it's just I woke up and you weren't in the bed next to me. I thought maybe you'd found a way to go home and left without saying goodbye first."

Duau leaned his forehead against hers. He smiled and shook his head. "I'd never leave you like that, Darcie." He brushed a kiss across her lips before he straightened. "I only thought to let you sleep. My body only requires two hours of sleep. I know you needed much more than that. I got up and came down here so I wouldn't disturb you. At dawn I decided to sit outside and watch the sunrise."

She noticed Duau didn't have on the Egyptian kilt he'd worn when he'd first shifted from his lion form. He now had on a pair of jeans and a sweatshirt. "Oh. Where did you find those clothes? I know I don't have any men clothing in my closet."

"I managed to work the box in the living room that plays pictures. After I watched it for a bit, I realized my kilt wouldn't be appropriate to wear in the mortal realm. So I willed the proper clothes onto myself before I went outside."

Darcie looked Duau up and down, thinking he'd done an excellent job on the clothes. The tight blue jeans hugged his body in the most delicious way. The sweatshirt did nothing to hide the thick muscles on his arms and chest.

"The box is called a television. So you spent the rest of the night watching TV while I slept?"

He nodded. "Mostly. I've learned a lot about the mortal realm from it. I also looked at the painting you did of me earlier in my lion form."

She bet he had learned a lot. She had satellite TV since she couldn't get cable up at the lake. Darcie could just imagine Duau had a hay day with some of the channels her dish picked up.

"Did you like the painting?" she asked reluctantly. Her ex would have probably told her it wasn't any good.

Duau put his arm around her shoulders and led her over to where the painting sat on the easel. He turned her to face it as his gaze ran over the canvas. "I love it. You perfectly captured me in my lion form. I have a very talented mate."

Darcie felt her cheeks flush with pleasure. "I'm glad you like it. Would you let me paint you again? This time as you are now. Not as the lion."

"Of course you can paint me anytime you wish, however you wish."

A smile tugged at Darcie's lips. "You may regret saying that. I actually want to paint you in a couple ways then. The first will be of you outside on the deck with the lake as the backdrop." She suggestively ran her gaze over Duau's body. From the heated look he gave her in return, she felt he'd be more than willing to pose for the second painting she had in mind. "The second one, I want to paint you nude."

He put his arms around her waist and pulled her to him as he pressed the erection he sported against her. "I have no objections posing nude for you. How about you start with that one first?"

Darcie shook her head and chuckled. "Nice try. Since it's still early enough, and while the light outside is good, I want to paint you out on the deck first. Then later tonight

I'll start on the nude. That one may take a couple days to finish I'm guessing."

She'd be lucky to finish it even in that timeframe. Darcie had a feeling painting Duau nude she'd get a bit on the distracted side. It'd be next to impossible for her to see that magnificent body of his stretched out before her naked and not touch or taste it.

Duau sighed dramatically. "If you insist. And here I've been thinking of all the things I wanted to do to that delectable body of yours once you woke up."

It was tempting, but the number of good days to paint outside would be few and far between soon. She lightly smacked Duau's chest. "I'm the artist here, buddy. I decide what I want to paint. Now let me go so I can put on some clothes. The faster I get dressed and make myself a cup of tea, the faster we can get started outside."

"No need for you to go upstairs to get changed," Duau said. He released her and took a small step back. With a wave of his hand, her bathrobe came to be replaced with jeans and a sweat top that perfectly fit Darcie.

Darcie looked down at the clothes Duau had willed onto her body. She nodded before she gazed at him. "Not bad at all. I could get used to this. I hope you don't mind if I end up getting paint on them."

"I can always get you more. Now hurry up and make your tea. I'll move the easel and your paints outside for you while you do that." Duau turned her around and gave her a little shove in the direction of the kitchen. He also gave her a pat on the bottom for good measure.

Duau carefully move all the things she needed to paint as she waited for the kettle to boil. So far, he was the complete opposite of her ex-husband when it came to her painting. That alone made Duau the better man. She didn't want to let him go, not even for a minute. How could she keep him? Their worlds were so different. He was an Egyptian god. He'd live forever. She, on the on the other hand, would eventually grow old and die. He'd remain the same, forever young.

Darcie poured herself a cup of tea and then headed outside to the deck where Duau sat waiting for her in one of the patio chairs. He must have sensed her mood, because the smile he wore slowly faded. He held his hand out to her. Once she took it, he pulled her down so she sat across his lap. He took her cup of tea and placed it on the patio table before he snuggled her against his chest with her head resting on his shoulder. He put his arms around her.

"What's the matter, Darcie? Why do you look so sad all of a sudden?"

"I just realized how much you mean to me, Duau. How can I let you go? I think you've spoiled me for other men."

A loud cat growl rumbled out of his chest. He lifted her so she sat up straight on his lap and then cupped her face in his hands. "There will be no other men in your life, Darcie. Only me. I'm your mate. I've claimed you as my own."

"Then what will become of us? I know you have to return to the underworld. That you have to find your brother. Can it seriously work? I'm just a mortal, and you're an Egyptian god. Is it possible?"

"We'll work it out as we go, Darcie. Like you, I don't intend to ever let you go."

"I hope you'll feel the same way when I'm old and wrinkly," she said in return.

"I'd still love you even if you were old and wrinkly, but that isn't going to happen."

"Of course it's going to happen, Duau. I'm mortal, remember?"

"You won't be for very much longer if I can help it."

Darcie sat up straighter on his lap. "What do you mean? Are you able to make me immortal?"

"I can't, but one of the other gods can. My brother and I

only have the ability to take away the marks of death from the body of the dead when they come seeking entrance to the underworld. I want you to be my mate in every sense of the word. For you to be that you need to be immortal. Besides, I'm a possessive man when it comes to you, and I have no intention of allowing even death to take you from me."

She swallowed around the lump that had suddenly formed in her throat as Duau spoke. "I'm going to just blurt this right out before I lose my nerve to say it. I love you, Duau. I never believed in love at first sight, or that there is that perfect someone out there for someone, but it's all true when it comes to you."

Duau cupped the back of her head and brought her lips down to his. He kissed her slowly, he nipped and sucked at her mouth until she moaned with her growing hunger. He soon pulled away. "We're mates, Darcie. We should fall in love with each other the instant we meet. That's the way it works. I love you as well." He shifted her on his lap so the hard length of his cock was against her bum. Darcie bit back a moan as her pussy tightened in response. "Now hurry up and drink your tea. If you still want to paint me out here, you'd better get started pretty soon or I may be forced to change your mind about doing the nude second instead of first."

CHAPTER SIX

O nce Darcie stood in front of the blank canvas, she became totally absorbed in her work. In no time at all the likeness of Duau, sitting on her deck with the lake in front of him and woods in all its fall glory to one side of him, took shape. He patiently sat for hours, and didn't complain about having to sit still.

After she finally put down her paintbrush, Darcie thought she'd managed to capture Duau's essence. She wiped her hands on a rag as he came to stand next to her. "It's basically finished. I may add a few more things to it, but that can be done later."

"It's perfect."

"Let's just say I'm greatly inspired by my model."

Duau went to open the sliding glass door for her so she could take the painting inside to dry. He brought the rest of her supplies into the house. "I can hear your stomach growling," he said. "Eat something. I'll wait upstairs for you."

He disappear upstairs with her easel tucked under one arm and the small table with her paints easily carried in his other hand. She'd thought to have him pose nude down on the couch, but obviously Duau had other ideas.

After she slapped together a quick sandwich and then ate it, Darcie headed up to join Duau. The sight of him totally naked, stretched out on her bed with his hands under his head, practically made her mouth water. She ran her gaze over his bronzed skin and muscular body. She didn't know if she'd even be able to paint, let alone form a coherent thought, with all that bared flesh within her sight. He rolled onto his side with his head on his ben arm. She dropped her gaze to his cock, which was hard and full as it stood at attention. She licked her dry lips.

"Is this pose all right with you?" Duau asked as he stared heatedly back at her.

"Um, that's fine."

Darcie put the blank canvas she'd brought upstairs on the easel and then picked up a charcoal pencil. Her blood surged as her nipples tightened beneath her shirt. Her pussy ached, wanting to be filled with Duau's cock. She'd painted nudes before, both women and men, but she'd always been able to distance herself from the male models while she'd painted. They'd just been a body, something for her to paint onto a canvas. With Duau as her male nude model, that wasn't the case. Her hand shook with longing as she drew his outline.

With grim determination, Darcie made herself focus on the upper half of Duau's body first. As she worked, she found herself more attuned to him than to what she drew. Once she had his upper body finished, she dropped her gaze. The air left her lungs in a *whoosh* as if someone had punched her in the stomach.

Duau had wrapped a large hand around his straining erection. Slowly, he pumped it up and down. Her gaze shot back up to his face. His lips were slightly parted and he breathed heavily. His eyes drifted shut as he pleasured himself. Her pussy clenched, and leveled her gaze back down to his cock. The sight of him working his thickness caused wetness to drip from her pussy to soak her panties. She licked her lips as a bead of moisture appeared on the head of his shaft.

Unable to concentrate anymore, Darcie wiped the charcoal from her fingers and then came around to stand next to the bed. Duau's eyes darkened with desire. She grabbed the bottom of her shirt and pulled it over her head. Just as quickly, she took off her jeans. Her bra and panties disappeared, and he opened his arms for her. She didn't hesitate to climb onto the bed next to him and slip into his embrace.

With a shove on Duau's shoulder, Darcie made him lie on his back. She pushed her tongue into his mouth as he claimed her lips in a kiss. It was her turn to kiss and lick every inch of his body as he'd done to her. Moving from his lips, she kissed a line across his jaw to his ear. She swirled her tongue inside it before she took the lobe between her teeth and gently bit. He purred softly and pressed his cock against her stomach.

Darcie continued her downward path. She shifted lower on his body, pressing kisses across his broad chest and down to his flat nipples. There, she sucked each tiny bud into her mouth, then dragged her teeth against them. Duau groaned loudly.

His stomach muscles rippled when she licked across his well-defined abs. Darcie shifted so she straddled Duau's thighs. She looked up to find him watching her intently with his eyes glazed in passion. With a firm grip on his cock, she swirled her tongue along the head. He moaned and lifted his hips off the bed. She swirled her tongue around him once again before she dragged it from base to tip along his shaft. His cock jerked with each swipe.

Opening her mouth, she took as much of his cock inside as she could manage. She closed her lips around him and sucked. Duau's groans filled the room. He threaded one hand through her hair, holding her to him. He hardened even more when she pumped her hand up and down the length she couldn't take inside her mouth.

Soon Duau tugged at her hair. "Enough. I want to be inside you when I come."

Darcie let go of his cock and then straddled his hips. With her hands resting on the mattress on either side of Duau's head, she rubbed her slick pussy along his shaft until she'd coated him with her juices. He reached between them and wrapped his hand around the lower part of his cock. Rising on her knees, she positioned herself above him and slowly took his cock inside her pussy. The feel of him filling her, stretching her, had her moaning with pleasure. Once she'd taken all of him, she lifted onto her knees again and then slowly pushed back down on him. The tip of her nipple brushed against his lips. He purred loudly, opened his mouth and sucked it deep inside. She felt the corresponding pull in her pussy.

She tightened her inner walls around him, and she increased her pace. She rode him faster. Her climax built inside her. Changing the angle of her hips, Darcie rubbed her clit against his thick shaft. Duau sucked harder on her nipple. Her core gripped his cock in a hard fist. She moaned as she fell over the edge into an intense orgasm.

As the last flutter of her climax faded away, Duau pulled out of her and then flipped her over onto her stomach. He took her by the hips and raised her onto her knees. With a cat's growl, he spread her legs apart with one muscled thigh and came to kneel behind her. The head of his shaft probed the entrance to her core. With both hands on her hips, he entered her from behind in one stroke. In this position she could take more of him. He reared back and slammed back into her. The tip of his cock butted up against her cervix. He continued to thrust into her as his cock hardened even more, stretching her to accommodate him. Darcie pushed back on him with each stroke in.

Duau rode her faster, leaned over her and bit her on the back of her neck where her shoulder and it met. Holding her in place with his teeth, he reached around their bodies until he found her clit. He rubbed the small nubbin of flesh while surging into her. With a cry of pleasure, her inner muscles clamp around his shaft, milking him. A loud growl filled the room. He sank into her one more time before he filled her with his cum.

Their bodies still joined, Duau shifted so he lay spooned against her back and held her close. Darcie's eyes fluttered shut. Since she hadn't had much sleep during the night, she let her body relax against him and fell asleep.

CHAPTER SEVEN

Duau moved Darcie's hair aside and licked the bite mark he'd put on the back of her neck. When he'd taken her from behind, the lion part of him had joined with the man. The lion wanted to mark her as his mate. Even though he didn't need to sleep, he was quite content to hold her in his arms as she slept. She fit perfectly in his embrace.

Each time they made love the closer they became. Duau couldn't picture how he'd survived all these centuries without Darcie. The prospect of having to return to the life he'd known before coming to be there held no appeal. Somehow he'd have to figure out how he could keep her and perform his duties as guardian to the gates of the underworld.

Thoughts of the underworld had him once again wondering what had happened to his brother. They'd never really been apart since the day of their birth. They'd always been able to communicate with each other telepathically. The absolute silence bothered Duau. He'd been lucky to find Darcie when he'd first arrived in the mortal realm. He only wished Sef had been as lucky as he.

There was no telling what could have happened to his twin. He had to find Sef, and somehow find a way to return to the underworld.

Darcie stirred in his arms. She turned so she lay facing him. With a finger, she smoothed it across his brow. "I hope it isn't thoughts of me that have you scowling like that."

Duau took her finger and nipped the tip before he pressed her hand to his chest. "No, it isn't thoughts of you that have me worried. I'm worried about Sef."

"I take it you two are very close."

"Very. We're identical in every way."

"Identical twins, uh? Hopefully when I finally get to meet Sef I don't mistake him for you and grab him where I shouldn't."

He slapped Darcie on the ass. "You better be able to tell us apart or I'll be very insulted."

"I'm sure the first time I kiss him by mistake I'll be able to tell he isn't you." She let out a little squawk as he hit her again. "I'm joking," she told him with a laugh.

"I know. I just used it as excuse to smack that shapely bottom of yours."

"At least you aren't scowling anymore." Darcie kissed Duau's chin. "I have to ask because I've wondered about this. I know you and Sef make up the Egyptian god Aker, but how did you come by your own names?"

"It's simple really. In Egyptian my name means tomorrow and Sef means yesterday. I guard the gate Ra uses to leave the underworld at the end of each night, which is the start of a new day. Sef guards the gate Ra enters at the beginning of each night, which is the end of the day."

"I get the tomorrow and yesterday now. You're going to have to return to the underworld aren't you, Duau?"

"Yes, but when I do go, it won't be for very long. I promise. Once I find Sef, I'll work out a way for me to be with you."

"You'd better or I may have to smack your butt."

Duau smiled. "Maybe I'd like that."

"Oh, a kinky Egyptian god, are we?"

"I'm willing to try new things."

"Good to know for future reference. For now, let's stick with what we both enjoy."

Duau soon lost the ability to think as Darcie reached down and took his cock in her hand.

* * * *

Darcie found the time she spent with Duau the happiest in a very long time. He never criticized her work, never made demands on her. She could just be herself. The more time she had with him the memories of her life with her ex-husband started to fade. She now had new memories of Duau to replace them.

Somehow she managed to finish most of the nude painting of Duau. It'd taken until late into the night since her concentration seemed to fly out the window after a short period of time. It'd also been a first for Darcie to paint while naked. Putting clothes on only to have to remove them shortly after she started to paint seemed a waste of time to her. At one point during the night, in between painting and lovemaking, they'd gone downstairs so she could get something to eat. He'd turned on the television while she'd cooked a meal for herself. She'd joined him while she ate.

They spent the next day outside, wandering around the woods or sitting out on the rocks next to the lake. They talked about everything and anything. Darcie told Duau about her first marriage, and how when her divorce had come through, she'd decided to buy her house on the lake. He'd told her stories of him and his brother, and what it was like in the underworld.

Now night time, they sat cuddled together on the couch as a fire blazed in the fireplace. The nights had gotten quite cold. The winter months set in earlier up north than it did in other places. Darcie had always grumbled about the cold, but with Duau there to snuggle against, she didn't find it quite the hardship she usually did.

Once the fire burned low, Darcie climbed off the couch. "I'd better get some more wood from the shed before the fire goes out."

"Do you need me to help?" Duau asked as he followed her to the front door.

"No, I can manage. I'll only be a few minutes."

Darcie slipped on her running shoes and then crossed the yard to the shed that sat not far from the house. She saw her breath in the air as she breathed. As she reached the shed, she looked back at the house to see Duau stood in the open doorway, watching her. She blew him a kiss and then opened the shed. A large stack of wood lay piled against one wall. She grabbed a couple split logs from the pile and then turned to hurry back inside.

Thinking of how good it'd feel to warm up in Duau's arms, Darcie had just about made it to the shed door when a man suddenly appeared in front of her. In the dim light that came from the lights outside, she couldn't make out much of his features, but his eyes glowed an eerie red that had her slowly taking a step back.

"What do you want?" she asked.

He followed her and sniffed the air. "I can smell the lion on you. He's taken you for his mate. I had orders to finish the lion off when our leader didn't return from taking care of his twin, but I think losing you will hurt the lion more."

The man pulled a sword out of thin air, and Darcie screamed Duau's name. A loud lion's roar sounded in the night. She suddenly knew this had to be a demon like the ones who'd attacked Duau and his brother in the underworld. The glowing red eyes were a dead giveaway.

She tried to block the sword that swung in her direction with one of the split logs she carried, but the demon knocked it easily out of her hands. Just before Duau reached the shed, the demon stabbed her through the stomach, and the blade came out the other side. Gasping in pain and shock, Darcie crumpled to the ground once the demon pulled his sword free.

Her life's blood slowly pumping out of her, Darcie watched Duau shift into his lion form on the fly as he burst into the shed. With a roar, he pounced on the demon. In a matter of seconds, the demon lay dead with his throat torn out.

Darkness slowly started to descend as Duau shifted back to human form and then scooped her up into his arms. He raced to the house, but Darcie knew he could do nothing for her.

"It's too late, Duau," she barely managed to whisper.

"No. I won't let you go."

Duau placed her onto the kitchen floor and used a couple tea towels to press against her wounds. Her body slowly going numb, she didn't feel the pain. Just before everything went black, Darcie whispered, "I love you" to Duau. The last thing she heard was his roar of pain.

* * * *

As the darkness engulfed her, Darcie felt herself fall. She couldn't hear or see anything. Then everything came to a stop. The darkness slowly receded until she found herself in a cavern of some sort. The only light came from a couple fire-lit torches set in the rock walls. She turned in a circle, wondering where exactly she was. When she came to face a large iron-banded door, she stiffened.

Darcie stepped closer to the man who stood in front of it. "Duau?" She shook her head. Now that she had a better look at him, she knew it wasn't her mate who watched her closely. He may look exactly like Duau, but she just knew it wasn't him. "Sef?"

Sef looked her up and down, taking in her bloodstained clothes. "You know Duau?"

"Yes. He's my mate."

"What happened? Is my brother unharmed?"

"A demon came. He said when his leader didn't return from supposedly taking care of you, he'd been ordered to take down Duau. The demon decided it'd hurt Duau more to take me away from him." Darcie blinked back tears. "Duau said he'd ask one of the other gods to make me immortal. I guess it's a little too late for that now."

Sef shook his head. "No, it isn't. Tell me where to find Duau, and everything will be all right. What's the name of my brother's mate?"

"I'm Darcie. Duau is at my house in Muskoka, in Canada. I'm dead. How can everything be okay?"

Sef smiled. "Ra will make this right, just as he did for me and my mate. Just wait and see. Through you I now can find Duau." He kissed her gently on the forehead. "Welcome to the family, my sister."

Darcie blinked as Sef disappeared.

* * * *

Duau held Darcie's lifeless body as silent tears dripped down his face. He'd never shed a tear in his life until now. Even though he knew they wouldn't bring her back to him he couldn't stem the flow. He buried his face in the crook of her neck and rocked her.

"Duau?"

Hearing his brother's voice, Duau's head shot up. He should have felt relieved to see Sef, but he felt nothing. "She's gone, Sef. I only had her for a short time."

Sef came to kneel beside him. "I saw Darcie. It's only because of her that I knew where to find you."

"She's in the underworld?"

"She's waiting at the gate."

"Why didn't you let her in?"

"Because I want my brother to keep his mate as I got to keep mine."

Duau shook his head. "I don't understand."

"I too found my mate in the mortal realm. The leader of the demons found us and tried to take her away from me. Ra gave Chandra her life back, and made her immortal. He'll do the same for you, Duau. All you have to do is ask."

"Ra," Duau called out. "You gave Sef back his mate. I ask that you do the same for me."

It shall be done, Duau. As I told your brother, you still will have your duty to the underworld. At night you will guard the gate, but during the day you may spend it with your mate. I give her back her life, and the gift of immortality.

As Ra's presence receded, Duau looked down at Darcie. She drew in a large gulp of air as her eyes fluttered open. He pulled away the towel from her wounds and found them gone as if they never were. He put his hand over her heart. It thumped strong beneath his palm.

"Duau? Am I really back?" Darcie asked as she looked about the room.

"Yes, you're back. Thanks to Ra."

Sef stood. "I'll leave you two alone, but I'll return with my mate tomorrow. I'm sure Chandra will be happy to meet Darcie." He disappeared.

Duau picked Darcie up into his arms and kissed her soundly. As he took her upstairs, he silently thanked Ra for giving him back the other half of his soul. Without her, life wouldn't have been worth living. Now that he had her back, he intended to show her how much she meant to him, even if he had to do it all night long.

The End

ABOUT THE AUTHOR

Marisa Chenery was always a lover of books, but after reading her first historical romance novel she found herself hooked. Having inherited a love for the written word, she soon started writing her own novels.

She now writes young adult books and erotic romances.

Marisa lives in Ontario, Canada, with her boyfriend, Steve, four children, four grandchildren (she's a young grandma in her fifties) and rabbit and dog.

www.marisachenery.com